Dark Days: The Monster Within

By Victor Ward

To Caiden and Owen, who both inspire and terrify me
in equal measure

Victor Ward Books. Dark Days: The Monster Within.

978-1-7343590-1-5 . Ebook Edition.

Dark Days, Darker Nights: The Monster Within

In the in dense jungle-like growths of the Fey Wilds stalked the Beast. Large and dominant, it was a prime example of its kind. A custom gene-engineered killer from the insane laboratories of the Fey. The Beast had been bred for the most impressive of their laboratory-arenas. Hate and hunger were its only driving emotions. Hate for the beings that had created and then discarded it. Hunger to continue this desperate existence in the Fey Wilds; the deadly dumping grounds for failed experiments of its former masters. Everything here was or had been one of their creations. Everything here had been designed to survive and kill in a manner pleasing to its creators. 12-Alpha fought every day to be one of those survivors who lived to the next sunrise.

A sudden burst of movement ahead grabbed

12-Alpha's attention. The tiny vibrations from something miniature and scurrying in the underbrush reached the sensitive drum like organs behind its forehead, speaking of possible prey. Complicated programming had been fed into its brain as an embryo calculated the weight, size and potential caloric value of the target. This meal would not be much, but the killing act alone would allow 12-Alpha to vent some of the seething rage the roiled inside. The Beast bent back the leaf-like flaps along its body which served as camouflage and dipped all 6 of its limbs down towards the ground. The lipless face peeled back over double-rows of razor-sharp fangs. A quick re-calculation of the prey's location, its potential escape vectors, and the beast leapt, aiming straight for the prey's likeliest location.

There was a flash and the hard pain of a sudden impact as 12-Alpha reached the Apex of its leap. Everything shifted away suddenly and the beast was no longer airborne or able to find the familiar jungle environment that had been its home a mere moment before. Instead, everything around 12-Alpha was plastic and metal and confining, with a faint burning smell in the air. The shriek of something to its right told 12-Alpha it wasn't alone in this new confirmed environment. Panicking, 12-Alpha swiped at the other being with five long reinforced claws.

When in doubt, kill everything.

DarkDays_MonsterWithin

Chapter 1

The landscape outside the reinforced glass window passed swiftly by with each mile. I watched the trees and scrub-brush with a detached eye as the transport van continued driving down the lonely highway. Where once at the start of our journey had stood the familiar oaks and pine trees of the American Midwest, the strange greens and purples of the alien-hybridized trees of the West Coast had become more and more commonplace. The trees had also grown thicker and closer together, until the view became one great forest only broken by the occasional dirt road or security-fenced farming collective. I'm told the west coast was once mostly dried grass and isolated farms, but the old habitat had not existed for many years now. Things had changed a little over ten years ago when the very fabric of our reality started tearing like a cheap cheesecloth in places, opening holes into other realities and letting all manner of weird, wonderful, and often horrifyingly deadly things spill out. The towns and cities of the world had come under siege from those things and we went from an open a sprawling civilization to one that locked the doors at night and fenced our communities like we had once fenced our yards. Once, those changes hadn't seemed real, living in a big city where rift events and their consequences were the province of new stories and urban legends. If I had known how completely a rift would change my life, I would have paid more attention.

My focus drifted to the badge in my hand. The badge was all solid steel and brass worked together in a weighty lump which screamed of more authority and responsibility than I had ever had in my life. The front of the badge depicted a pair of crossed spears and an ancient balance with the words 'ExoReality Containment Agency' hammered out in raised lettering along the top. Below the crossed spears my name had been stenciled in dark lacquer. Cut deep enough that I could feel the ridges was the name 'Marcus Black'. Having that name, my name, engraved there meant everything to me. Once I had been on the very opposite side of the law, fearing and hating pieces of metal very much like this one. Six years of hard work, four years in the academy, where I had spent twice as much time studying, training, and learning as any of my colleagues. Six years in which I had completely reinvented myself from a poor, semi-educated street kid to the focused and driven ExoReality Academy student who had managed to shed his past and adapt to a new future. I wasn't the scared kid from before the rifts changed my life, but I didn't yet feel like the law officer I was supposed to be. I was caught inbetween, like a shy adolescent at his first school dance, uncertain if he should be there and wondering if it was too late to run like hell back the way I had come. There was a rumble in the back of my head and I was reminded why running back home wasn't an option. There was no going back with this thing now lived within my skull and shared my body. My condition as one of the 'void-touched' wasn't ever going to go away any more than the terrible things memories of what had occurred afterwards. No, there was no 'back home' for me now, but with a lot of hard work, there might be a path forward.

My deep but probably incredibly sexy brooding was interrupted by a voice cheerful enough to summon small forest animals over a five-block radius, "Hard to believe you finally got your badge, right? Like it must be a dream or something."

I looked up from my hands. Originally the van had held a dozen of my fellow academy graduates headed out on their first assignment, but the numbers had dwindled down to only three of us while I had alternated between brooding and dozing. The suspiciously cheerful speaker was a woman of medium height and an African complexion who wore her uniform like she had been born into it. Her hair was a tightly packed set of curls only a couple of inches out from her head, below which was a pair of golden eyes with an intense focus, as if constantly in thought even as they bore straight at you. Like me, her uniform was freshly off the rack and a brass and steel badge like my own shone over her left breast. The woman stared at me intently, as if I was less a fellow officer and more a unique specimen she had run across in a lab. The silence as we stared at each other stretched out for an awkward moment and I tried to recover. I waved a hand in the air as though the silence was a fly buzzing around my head, "Yeah. I suppose so. Up until we got into the van I kept expecting someone to pop up and tell me I was missing an exam or something and would need to wait another year." I thought internally, or they'd changed their mind about my criminal record.

The other officer laughed. "If my scene forensics instructor could have, she probably would have done it in a heartbeat." She stuck out her hand. "There is only two of us left, so I'm guessing you are going to be the other junior detective in Mhanke Heights. We might have shared a firearms class together. My name is Olivia and this quiet piece of trouble next to me is my little sister, LittleBird."

I shook Olivia's hand. "Marcus Black. I think you are right about the class. With Seargeant Weld."

I glanced at the teenager sitting next to Olivia. Her skin contrasted sharply with my fellow officer, a pale complexion against Olivia's darker one. The kid had long straight hair which attempted to cover a truly impressive network of surgical scars across her skin. The teenager's focus was deep into her handheld tablet and I wouldn't have put the two of them together if they hadn't been sitting so close. I couldn't help but wonder if I had heard Olivia correctly. "Sisters?"

Olivia beamed. "Yep - and don't feel awkward. The skin tone throws most people off. Did you read the briefing on Mhanke Heights?"

I turned a little red, and rubbed at the back of my head. "I have the papers, but I can't read them."

The admission earned me a quizzical expression, those contemplative eyes working in overdrive as she worked out the meaning of my response. "You can't read? I thought literacy was a requirement to be in law enforcement."

I shook my head. "I'm literate, but I can't actually see the words on the paper."

Her facial expression didn't change. After a moment's further hesitation, I removed my sunglasses and let Olivia see my eyes.

LittleBird must have kept an eye on us while playing with her tablet, because she dropped the device with an audible clunk as it hit the floor. Olivia on the other hand didn't flinch, which was damned impressive. I should probably explain; my eyes are the most visible part of my no longer quite human condition. I haven't had human eyes for at least 5 years now. Where once had been the blue and white colors of a normal human eyeball, now there was nothing but a deep dark inky black orb. People who had seen them had alternately described these eyes as 'buglike', 'creepy', and 'demonic'. None of those descriptions was strictly correct, but they weren't far off either.

Olivia tilted her head and continued to study me. "Are you blind?"

I had expected to get at least a flinch from the fellow graduate and was quietly impressed by her lack of reaction. I had been expecting my agency coworkers would need time to get used to my 'condition' but she wasn't phased at all. I decided to press my luck and said, "I'm not blind, strictly speaking. My eyes don't have light receptors like everyone else. Whatever I have instead can see the depth and distance of something way better than most people and can see several things the human eye cannot. In addition to coming in the fetching color of cheap b-movie monster black, they don't detect color at all. If something isn't raised on the surface so I can see the depth of it, it might as well be blank. I'm useless with computer screens...and printed paper."

Olivia nodded as if it made sense to her. Impressive again, since it didn't make sense to me and they were my eyeballs. "Is that related to why you have the IWP patch?"

I gathered myself to give a full explanation, but was saved by the crackle of the passenger compartment intercom. The static-laden voice of the driver came over the speaker, stress audible in his tone over the interference of the speaker. "You guys better come out and look at this. We have a downed vehicle off the road."

Chapter 2

Olivia and I shared a brief glance before diving for our kits. Vehicles traveling alone these days was rare, aside from heavily armored vans like the one we rode in. Anything and everything could happen out in the wide spaces between cities and if you weren't part of a convoy, there might not be anyone who could come along and help you. A car crash could be a simple mechanical breakdown, but it might mean something more concerning had occurred. I locked eyes with Olivia; this normally would be a matter for the local police or the heavily understaffed highway patrol, but we were first on the scene. Olivia picked up her kit and checked her firearm, a surprisingly sizable revolver. She went out the back of the van first, with me following close behind. The driver and his partner had also left the vehicle with their guns drawn. They took up positions on either side of the vehicle and would cover us in case whatever danger had forced the car of the road was still present. I could feel the tenseness across my shoulders as I pulled my own pistol and covered Olivia as she approached the car.

Olivia gave the standard greeting as she

approached the side of the vehicle. "ERC response. Do you require assistance?"

The vehicle was a tiny 4 door compact, with a chipped Ford symbol splashed across the rear. The driver side door was completely missing and there were cracks along the front windshield. Burnt tire tracks led from a hole in the road straight to where the car rested in a shallow ditch. Whatever had happened to the car, it had occurred quickly and with a great amount of violence. Olivia gave me an all-clear and I approached the vehicle.

The inside of the vehicle was worse than the outside. Deep gouges and scratches lined the interior and a spray of blood had splashed across the windshield. The driver's seat was almost entirely missing and there was no sign of whoever had been in the seat when the attack occurred. A woman's corpse lay strapped into the passenger seat, her face in a rictus of shock. The slick sheen of viscera and blood shown through the three deep gouges which crossed her chest. I only hoped she had died quickly.

Olivia grimaced and turned her face towards mine. "Given the hole in the road, I'd want to guess they crashed trying to avoid a rift, but this appears to be some kind of attack. Did something come out of the ground and chase them?"

I surveyed the hole in the road. "There was definitely a rift here. I can see the mana concentration from where it was leaking out while the rift was active."

Olivia's face was outright skeptical. "You can see it?"

I nodded. My eyes may have been useless with writing, but there was a bright swirl of pinkish-purple mist slowly moving away from about 3 feet off the ground above the hole. I recognized the traces of a mana spillover. "When rifts occur, mana from the other reality dumps into this one like water down a drain. From the dispersal, I'd say it happened within the past couple hours. Mana might not have been the only thing to get pulled over however."

She asked, "Something big enough to attack a car driving at speed?"

I cocked my head. "Or someone. Some things that come through the rift are sentient."

She blew a low whistle. "Great. What do you think happened to the driver?"

I glanced about. "I don't see any signs of a body. Let's call it in and see if we can figure out who these poor bastards were." I looked over at the van driver, who was slowly lowering his firearm. "Hey, how far away are we from Mhanke Heights?"

He glanced down the road, as if he could see

the town beyond his vision. "About 10 minutes out. I called in the accident; do we have anything to update them with?"

I waved a hand towards the downed car. "Tell them it was a Rift Event. Call a Code ER-6, something alive might have come through."

That got the driver's attention, and he motioned for his partner to mount back in the truck. I turned around and opened my kit, rooting around for latex gloves. Olivia was already popping open the back of the vehicle, so I went around the passenger side to get at the glovebox. Belatedly, I realized I hadn't turned my bodycam on and cursed softly - having the recorder active during an investigation was agency 101. I had opened the glove compartment when I realized what it was I was doing. I was *investigating*. I hadn't yet reported in to the headquarters and I was already arms deep in a major rift event investigation. Hopefully my new boss, Captain Al-Radke, liked people with initiative. I couldn't read any of the papers I pulled out of the glovebox, but that was not going to stop me. I had been embarrassed to use my little 'helper' on the van ride, but there wasn't room for such sentimentalities now. Trying not to think about what my partner would feel about it, I opened my smartphone and issued a quick voice command to activate the Image Identifier application. A friend of mine had built the application for cases like mine as well for more traditionally blind folks trying to live in a brailleless world. Once the application beeped to let me know it was active, I passed the smartphone's camera over the first paper.

It beeped and gave me the results verbally. "Picture."

I rolled my eyes. "Describe Object."

"Two subjects. One male in gray suit, female in white dress."

It was a crap description, but the AI wasn't very useful with anything other than raw text. I put the picture aside. Olivia could look at it later and give me a better answer. I moved to the second item, a plastic card, and hit pay dirt.

The smartphone chirped. "Card, Identification."

I repeated the 'describe object' command. The smartphone took a moment and then spit out what data it could determine. "State Driver's License. ID is D211234. Name is Frank Owens. Age is 26. Address is..."

I devoured the information and informed the application to save the readout and a picture of the license. The rest of the papers consisted of the usual mix of outdated registration cards and insurance paperwork, all under the name Frank Owens. I started filing the papers into an evidence bags as I called out to Olivia.

"I think I've identified the driver. Mr. Owens of Mhanke Heights. No mention of the woman so far, though."

Olivia came around the corner of the car holding a bridal veil. "I think they might be newlyweds. Almost all the stuff in back is hers and some of the paperwork lists her name as Eliza Barrens."

Ouch. They had probably been returning from the wedding when she had died. A whole hope-filled life ahead of her gone in one explosive instant. The other voice inside of my head, woke up and growled softly. It sensed we were looking at the work of another predator and the thing inside me hated the idea of competition.

I sighed outwardly as the growling built up as a pressure inside my skull. It was never a positive thing when my other half got interested. The thing inside me had a mean streak a mile wide and definite tendency to push me towards violence if not controlled. Another exciting facet of my condition. I passed the picture to Olivia. "Is that our victim?"

Olivia raised an eyebrow. "It is, but how did you know it was a woman if you couldn't see the picture?"

I waggled the phone. "Little technical help. Only way I was allowed into the agency."

Olivia was reaching for the phone to examine the application, when we heard a loud crack that resounded across the road. I turned around and saw our driver lying on the pavement. I was still mentally identifying the cracking sound as a firearm discharge when a burning pain ran across my arm, closely followed by several more of the cracking sounds. Training took over and Olivia and I dropped to the ground as more shots passed overhead. Someone was shooting at us.

Chapter 3

Shock was a heavy hand on my thoughts as I scrambled for cover. Bandits weren't unheard of outside the cities, but I couldn't think of a single good reason anyone would ambush a police unit in the open. The other voice in my head was screaming to attack. It saw the threat and railed to kill each attacker in the most direct way possible. My other half saw the incoming fire as a challenge to its authority and wanted to respond with the maximum amount of violence possible.

I wasn't going to give it the pleasure if I could avoid it. Instead, I pulled my sidearm, a solidly built 9-millimeter Rutger, and flipped the safety off. A person, no multiple people, stood or kneeled at the tree line, firing at us in a ragged line that hugged the trees wherever possible. Olivia drew her own sidearm, a massive revolver and sent a shot downrange. The resulting boom hurt my eardrums and a decently sized chunk of pine tree exploded, causing the man next to it to flinch and drop as wooden splinters flew into his side. The giant firearm barely moved in her hand as she fired again repeatedly, emptying the revolver but suppressing our opponents with a grim efficiency. As she reloaded the weapon, I reached into myself and gave my other half a little more access than I normally did. My vision became several factors more complex as the swirls of mana became overlaid with the bright sparks emanating from any decently sized living thing nearby.

I spoke quickly. "12 people along the tree line. 2 more flanking at 2 o'clock, headed to 3 o'clock."

I squeezed off several shots of my own, hitting one man right in the center the bright spark of his soul. He doubled over and didn't get back up. Jesus, I thought. I just killed someone. The other me celebrated the kill, but urged me to get closer to my targets. It wanted to feed on them, to let our claws and fangs sink into their flesh. My shoulder knotted up with each passing bullet and I was very aware the car we hid behind was nothing but cheap aluminum and fiberglass. It wouldn't stop a direct hit. I loosed another couple rounds at one of the men hugging a tree for cover. They dropped to the ground, but I wasn't certain if I had hit them or only made them dive for cover. This was getting intense.

Olivia stood unfazed by the incoming fire. She calmly reloaded the revolver and rose from her sitting position to send three more rounds downrange with a quick *Boom, Boom, Boom* of her pistol. An answering round hit her in the shoulder and she spun as her body hit the ground with an oopmh. I reached out a hand to pull her back into cover, but Olivia sat bolt upright and kept firing back. Another round entered her chest, but fly off with an audible ping sound like a rock bouncing off a tin roof. I wish I could say I didn't stand their gaping for a moment, but it is not every day you see someone take a shot and walk it off. There wasn't any blood, but I was fairly certain Olivia wasn't wearing a fancy new bulletproof vest. A quick glance over at the van showed the driver's partner had pulled him into the safety of the armored vehicle, who was taking maximum advantage of the bulletproof panels. I nodded me head over to the van. "Let's get out of here. I don't want to end up dead before I can report into work."

Olivia considered at the van the way someone might examine a stack of paperwork. She still didn't seem to be afraid of the massive number of bullets winging in the air overhead. "That's a lot of open ground, but you are right. I didn't bring enough bullets for this."

If we hadn't been in danger of imminent death, I would have rolled my eyes. The situation involved being outnumbered, outgunned, and needing to run across a couple hundred feet without cover and her sole concern was her ammunition count. Where in the hell did they find this woman? I decided to pretend I wasn't inches from pissing myself and gathered my legs under me for the sprint. "All right. On 3?"

Olivia nodded. "1. 2...3!"

We took off like a pair of olympic sprinters. Unfortunately, we only got a couple feet before the flankers I had completely forgotten about opened up and cut us down. At least one round had torn right into my lower leg and I kissed the dirt under the sudden sideways impact. Olivia had been closer to them than I had and took several rounds simultaneously, including one right to the side of the head. The bullet didn't travel through, but she dropped like a puppet with its strings cut. I rolled on my side casting about for my pistol. The ever-closer crunching of boots told me the attackers continued to advance, and I kept trying to find my firearm. My other half was screaming wordlessly in my head, demanding I give in and let it take over. I wasn't ready to surrender to my less controlled half yet. My pistol had to be somewhere nearby, but my blurred vision couldn't determine where it was. A sudden kick to my side rolled me on my back. I stared down the barrel of my attacker's rifle and knew I had run out of time.

<u>Chapter 4</u>

My blood pressure pounded as desperation flooded me. I didn't know where my sidearm was and if I had, I don't think I would have lived long enough to use the damn thing. My vision tunneled in on the barrel of a rifle slowly lined up with my forehead. The other voice inside of my head screamed for control, and may God forgive me, I gave into it. There was a scream of triumph in my skull as I unleashed my willpower and the strange, unnatural nature of the creature flooded into my flesh. It didn't push into my flesh the way a a real, physical thing did. Instead we became entangled, both inhabiting the same space, the same body. I felt impossible ripples under my flesh as my own body became something less real, something less a part of the natural world. Our voices merged and there was no longer Marcus Ward and his pet demon. Now there was only *Us*. We thought as one, we hungered as one.

The rifle barked, but hadn't been lined up properly, and our dodge to the side had brought it out of line with our head.

The bastard had dared to challenge us and we

responded in kind. A slap sent the rifle sprawling and we went for the attacker's throat. Blunt human fingers wrapped around the prey's windpipe and crushed it, leaving them choking in the dirt. Before his companion could react, we pounced upon the second prey, driving his soft skull against a rock. Beyond what any of our attackers could see, our form reached out in the universe and sought the soft energies binding the man's soul to the meat of his body. We ripped them out and the unconscious man screamed in an agony most human would never experience in their short lives.

We feasted. The soul itself may be immutable, but the anchors tying it to mortal flesh were sweetmeats for our consumption. A roar of exultation escaped our lips as the energy from the second man died and was added to our meal. We hadn't fed, not truly fed, since finding ourselves in this world and it was like cold water washing over desert sand. Another bullet passed into our corporeal form, but our flesh was no longer entirely anchored in reality and the impacted flesh only rippled as the bullet passed through it. Another challenge, another attempt to kill us. Our course was clear. Challengers would be killed or we would be killed meeting their challenge. This was the only law of the void. The only law that mattered.

We ran at the challengers, right across the open ground. More bullets ripped by our form, tearing at the edges. Repairing the damage was a simple task, but drained the fresh energy gained form our feeding. The human half pulled us into performing a zig zag pattern, making it harder for the prey's guns to aim at us. We leapt; feet propelled far higher than any normal human could have jumped. The enemy line broke in horror as we came down in front of them. One man dropped his firearm as he ran and we bounded after him. Unarmed prey would be the easiest to trap and consume.

STOP.

The command slammed against our consciousness like a brick. The human half of me wouldn't allow the killing of an unarmed attacker. The predator half of me pointed out that the very idea of letting them go was ludicrous. Challengers either killed or were killed. There was no other outcome. The unity between our minds ripped apart as we struggled with the conflict. The human side was strong, stronger than the other side, but it would get us killed over nothing if we let it.

STOP.

Another wave of will from our human mind slammed into our predator mind, and forced it down, away from control, splitting the unity we had enjoyed for such a brief amount of time.

There was feeling like a truck slamming to a halt and I snapped back into full control of my body with a wave of expelled breath. I could feel pain shooting up from where I had been grazed a half-dozen times. I screamed in frustration, still burning off the adrenaline of the firefight and the strong desire for violence still echoing in my head. I gazed down at my bloody hands. I had killed. Killed people with my bare hands. I hadn't killed anyone since I had been afflicted with my symbiotie and now, *now* I had killed two - no three men in less than an hour. It hadn't been an accident either. I had let the other part of me take control, using its enhanced speed and ability to avoid harm to turn the tables on my attackers. I compounded my damnation when I allowed myself to do exactly the dumb, direct assault the predator favored, almost getting shot a dozen times in the process. I had been scared and had given in, leaving two men to die in agony. Training said I should secure the scene and check on my comrades, but I put my head in hands and let my feelings wash over me.

Chapter 5

A couple minutes later I heard the shuffling of feet and looked up to see Olivia walking towards me. I bolted to my feet. "I thought you died."

Olivia shook her head, which clearly still had a neat hole in one temple. It occurred to me that the wound didn't have any blood coming from it. There wasn't blood from any of her wounds either. She gave me a quizzical look again and touched the hole in her temple. "Oh. No, but I was out for a little while. Bullet knocked my skull around but didn't penetrate."

I raised an eyebrow in response. "You have a bulletproof skull?"

Olivia shrugged her shoulders. "You aren't the only one with a 'condition'. The holes will fix themselves over the next couple hours. You didn't notice me giving you covering fire?"

"You could say I was a little single minded at the moment."

"I saw. I hadn't connected the dots before. You are a void touched."

Damn. I winced and peered down at my now-human hands. Void-Touched were people who had the terrible luck to be too close to rifts that opened into a world called 'The Void'. When people from here get dumped over there, normally they just go insane from being plopped into a place in which none of the physical laws apply. A small handful make it back sane. A smaller number make it back sane, but get stuck with a little hitchhiker in the back of their heads. Guess who luck was terrible enough to win that one in a million lottery? I didn't answer and avoided her gaze as motioned over at the van, where the driver was receiving first aid from his partner and LittleBird. "I am. My passenger is a low level Void predator. Likes to tell me what to do, but is too immature to do anything without my permission." *Usually,* I thought and suppressed a shudder.

Olivia was unfazed. "Explains the patch then, is that why your vision isn't normal?"

'The Patch' in question was a embroidered piece of fabric with the letters 'IWP' on my right breast. People with certain rift-related conditions deemed dangerous to the general public had to wear the issued patches at all times. *Innate Weaponized Personnel* was the government's official term for people like me. Part of my academy term had also involved two years of IWP 'control' training and 'testing' before I was allowed outside the bounds of the academy. I can't really blame the law. In the past, other void-touched had completely lost control and racked up an impressive number of dead civilians before being stopped. I was rather lucky mine wasn't a heavy swinger in their world, or otherwise I might have wound up with a bullet in my head long before I graduated academy. I was allowed out of the academy now, but only if I wore the patch at all times - my own Judea Star. For the millionth time I wish I had never encountered the Void Rift, but there's no helping what has already occurred. "Yeah, little bastard entered me via the eyes. Screwed them up and did his best to fix them once he realized he was stuck. Unfortunately, vision isn't quite the same concept on their realm as it is in theirs. No joy of internet cat videos or television watching since."

Olivia turned her eyes back towards the van. "Captain Al-Radke stated he'd be on his way. Want to help me survey the ground for any suspect casualties?"

I nodded my head. It was grim work, but anything that involved finding out why this had happened felt like a good idea. This had been an automobile accident, hadn't it? Then why had someone been so willing to kill over it?

Chapter 6

Olivia and I secured the scene as best we could, marking where three more of the suspects had been downed by gunfire in addition to the two people I had killed near the car. Each of the attackers was dressed in a wild array of leather jackets and at least one had a motorcycle helmet clipped to his belt. A biker gang, then. There was no sign of the bikes or where our attackers had fled to, although they had fallen back in the direction of the town itself. I couldn't help but feel like it was busywork, since nothing had turned up more information than what we already knew. We weren't going to find any maps to secret hideouts shoved in back pockets or other evidence beyond what was already found.

We were still documenting the carnage when we could see the local CSI van drive up with a patrol car behind it. An older gentleman I took to be Captain Mike Al-Radke got out of the patrol car and shook his head at the scene. Al-Radke was a tall, angular man with the hard-bitten look of someone who's seen more than his fair share of dark situations. He bore the easy grace of someone who had been doing this job for a while, and nearly everyone on the scene greeted him by his name, even ours drivers. He spent a few minutes in conversation with each person, gathering information from the Crime Scene Investigators, talking to the driver and then beckoning us over to the hood of the patrol car with an easy wave of his hand. The Captain had spread a map of Coastal County, where Mhanke Heights was located, out on his patrol car. His partner, a tall husky fellow with tosseled hair, leaned against the cruiser next to him, sipping a coffee. To my vision, this newcomer's body glowed with a truly impressive number of mana-tattoos. Mana-tattoos were a cutting edge technique in which preprogrammed 'spells' could be tattooed onto a person's body with a type of mana-conductive ink, needing only some tiny knowledge of spellcraft to activate as needed. Some of my fellow academy trainees had gotten a shield or stun spell inscribed as part of their personal kit, usually a one-off job designed to help when no other options were available. I'd never seen anyone go all in like this guy had. Al-Radke's partner must have had at least a dozen of the things inscribed on his flesh. I could not imagine how much it must have cost to get all the work done.

The partner caught me staring and rolled up a sleeve, unaware that I could already see the entirety of his skin art. He chuckled knowingly. "Spell Tattoos. Helps us mortals get a leg up when we need it in the field - and makes me look pretty dashing too."

I wrenched my eyes away from the glowing lines before it got too awkward. "My apologies. I've never seen so many on a single person before."

"You probably won't again. I hold the record around these parts. Think of me has a kind of hobbyist."

The captain cracked a smile. "What Chauncy here means to say is that he's a decent spell programmer who creates his own tattoos, and he's been sleeping with the owner of the local tattoo parlor who uses him as a big ol' guinea pig."

Chauncy snorted. "A guinea pig is not the only animal she uses me as."

I was a little surprised at the levity at first. I would eventually learn that when you work in law enforcement you have to find humor where you can get it, even if it's a couple hundred feet away from a corpse. Olivia offered her hand to the captain. "Junior Detectives Olivia and Marcus, reporting for duty sir."

The rookie formality drew a grin from the captain. "You can call me Mike when it's just the four of us. I'm sorry we don't have time for formal introductions but I'll keep it simple. I'm captain and head of this little department. Chauncey and I have been holding down the fort since the rifts first started happening out here several years ago, before the fence went up. It is rather clear at this point the rifts aren't going away any time soon and last year's surge put most of the west coast states in the 'high-incident' zone. Our job here is to keep people safe, stop them from killing each other in weird and interesting ways, while supporting the local police force as much as we can. You two did a professional job at getting the investigation here started and in keeping your heads once the ambush occurred. To start, I want a full rundown from each of you on what happened exactly as you remember it."

Olivia gave him her summary of events and I followed afterwards, only stumbling when I got to the two flankers firing at us as we ran. The captain listened attentively and then held up a hand when I had trouble getting the words out. "I prefer we be frank and honest inside this team. I'm guessing you *ate* them, which is why they their corpses are frozen in an expression of utter panic and terror."

That got Chauncey's attention and he dropped whatever was in his hands. I knew there was no defense for what I'd done. "I'm sorry sir, I didn't have another way out at the time."

Captain Al-Radke's expression stayed commanding, with no clues as to how he felt about my admission showing on his face. "You did what you had to. I wouldn't feel too negative about killing someone who is actively trying to kill you. What I do want to be certain is you don't go haring off after your attackers like that again. I was assured you had better control than I am seeing here."

I hope I hid my relief at his response, but it was probably written all over my face. "It won't happen again."

Mike Al-Radke simply grunted. "See that it doesn't. Did you two get a chance to examine the downed suspects?"

I was happy to change the subject and pointed out the evidence marker flags we had established. "They were wearing biker leathers and a mix of concealable weapons and pre-rift hunting rifles. Likely a convoy gang of some kind."

The captain nodded. 'The convoys often pay small armed groups to provide security. More than one biker gang has turned semi-legit doing escorts. Some are only using it as cover though."

I peered over at the highway turned battlefield. "I know convoys were a thing in Detroit, but how often do you get them out here?"

He waved a hand at the map. "Out here on the coast almost everything runs by convoy. That means two to three convoys arriving and a nearly equal number leaving every day. Most are bringing in the kind of sellable goods and supplies Mhanke Heights needs and taking out what arrives at the docks. Added to each one is a group of tagger-ons, people traveling or moving, internet retailers dropping off goods, a few camp followers who sell services to the convoy like food or automobile repair."

My eyebrows rose. "That's a lot of movement. How big are the convoys?"

The captain smiled thinly. "Oh about a dozen vehicles, not counting the larger ones who show up and stick around a few days. The state ExoReality Containment headquarters even sends a rotating convoy which runs between the county jurisdictions and the capitol on a three-week route. Picks up evidence, contraband and suspects for secure holding. It's like the old west outside the fence."

Olivia interjected. "It might be a place to start checking, but we still don't know why we were attacked. There's nothing in the car or our van worth taking a bullet over."

Chauncey scanned the scene of the car wreck. "Did you find the driver of the vehicle? Maybe he'll know more about why this went down."

I shook my head. "Not yet. It's possible whatever attacked the car took him with it or he headed to town on foot."

The captain took off his police cap and ran his hand over a small knit cap which sat under it. "I don't want to leave any civilians wandering those woods with nightfall coming. We'll ask captain Braugher of the police department to send someone to check the hospitals and the convoy rest stop for our other suspects. In the meantime, let's assume our driver took off on foot. We'll split into pairs and scout back towards town. If we are lucky, we'll either find our driver or some clues as to what might have made mincemeat out of the car. Olivia, you go along the road with Chauncey. We'll have someone escort your sister to headquarters. Marcus? You're with me."

Chapter 7

We headed out after a brief conference with the CSI and their police escort. The crime scene investigators assured us we'd be the first to know what they found once blood and hair samples were processed. It was strange pressing into the treeline around the highway. Back east ,almost all the wildlife had been the same Earth-native species which had been inhabiting the area for the past century, but out here on the coast the familiar faces of things often took a left turn. The trees had bark like their original pine forebears, but the leaves came in every shape and color a person could imagine. From 4-inch-long needles to complicated multi-part leaves with up to a dozen corners. One tree even had long vine-like tendrils which seemed to move and feel along the branches of the other nearby trees. Wildlife flitted across the branches, squirrel-like lizards with miniature vestigial wings and 4-legged spider bugs as big as dinner plates chasing tiny flying mammals.

I stopped at the remains of a mailbox jutting a few feet beyond the path. A tree had risen next to it, forcing the mailbox out at an odd angle. A family name, 'Golan', was still painted in red paint along the side. There had once been a home here, one of thousands upon thousands of suburban and rural homes which had been abandoned as the rifts forced people into cities and the alien species took things over. If I had come here as a kid, this would have been a busy suburb with normal families and normal cars and normal roads. It was all part of a world which no longer existed.

Mike Al-Radke seemed to notice my distraction. "I knew the Golans. They live on Auger street now. The whole family moved after a neighbor got caught in a rift event."

I rubbed at my badge. "I know a thing or two about how scary that can be."

Al-Rake rubbed his chin. "I wanted to talk to you about that. How far away was the rift that got you?"

"Maybe a dozen feet? I was driving a car at the time. I drove in and fell out later, got thrown into a guardrail."

"Detroit?"

"Yeah. Rifts were rare over there six years ago. Guess it wasn't my night."

He nodded and gazed distantly at the decayed foundations of what had been the Golan household. "There is an understatement. Still, I'm glad to have you. Chauncey and I have been swamped ever since the surge. How much has Victor told you about being a void-touched?"

I was surprised the captain would be familiar with my mentor. "You know Victor?"

He didn't elaborate, so I filed it away to ask later and instead answered his question. "Quite a bit I guess. He helped me figure things out, even helped me get into the academy as part of my IWP training."

"Did he tell you what feeding that thing inside you would do?"

I winced. "Yeah. He warned me the little bugger inside of me was probably immature, something like a juvenile. Feeding it would make it stronger, more able to push its will against mine."

"Did he tell you what would happen if it's will proved stronger than yours?"

I glanced around and replied bluntly. "Yes." This was a serious conversation, but something was niggling at the back of my head, prevent me from focusing entirely on the subject at hand.

If the captain noticed my hesitation, he didn't let it stop him. "Do you know how we found the second void-touched ever recorded?"

I tried to answer him, but whatever was nagging at me was taking up more and more of my attention. "I'm guessing a pile of bodies, an otherwise normal citizen trying to gnaw…"

I froze. It finally started to occur to me what was wrong. The birds had stopped singing. I couldn't hear any of the chittering or rustling noises that had followed our walk so far. I pulled within myself and expanded my sight to see the bright lights of living souls again. There should have been dozens of briefly flickering movements of animals nearby, but instead the forest was a grey blanket devoid of nearby life. Until I looked at the captain, and more importantly, beyond him.

Chapter 8

"Oh shit!" I yelped in a completely manly and non-hysterical manner.

The massive bush behind my captain wasn't a bush. As I reached for my firearm, the 'leaves' behind him stirred and the entire thing rose up into a beast of terrible size. The creature was the size of a medium-sized car, all green scales and leaf-like flaps. Massive claws tipped the end of cat-like paws and the thing had more teeth than any animal had a right to own. Then there were the eyes. They had round pupils like a person and they burned with a furious hatred only a thinking, sentient being was capable of. Death had waited while we talked, measuring the right time to end our lives.

My firearm was halfway to a firing position when it leapt. The captain must have seen my reaction or heard the beast rise, because he dropped flat on the ground and rolled, narrowly avoiding the landing claws of the monster. I fired at the creature point blank with my pistol, but the rounds did little more than leave thin bloody scratches on its forehead. The beast didn't hesitate before backhanding me across the space and right into the mailbox I had previously been examining. I hit the ground hard and could have sworn I felt a rib break. My other half reacted instantly and before I could think about it, we roared right back in its face. In retrospect, the roar was probably more akin to a mouse trying to stare down the cat, but there hadn't been time to consider the consequences of our actions. The beast roared right back, an echoing volume which was far stronger than anything human lungs could compare to. It raised a massive set of claws to end me right then and there when a series of sharp bangs echoed from my right.

Whatever the captain was packing, it was a lot more effective than my 9-millimeter. The beast roared in pain as bullets ripped into its hide from the captain's semiautomatic. I took the opportunity to indulge in the better part of valor by throwing myself to the side. Once I was clear, I moved to the other flank of the beast and added my own fire. The creature roared in anger, but hesitated in deciding which one of us to kill first. It eventually settled on me and turned with impressive speed, jaws opening wide for the kill.

That's when I apparently decided to do the second dumbest thing I'd done that morning. I ran right at it, sliding in the wet foliage at the last moment. The beast hadn't expected the maneuver and its teeth almost missed me completely, doing little other than shredding a uniform sleeve. By the strange mechanics of dumb luck, I ended up under the beast. Franticly dodging its feet as it searched for me. The good news was that I wasn't dead yet. The bad news was that I was looking at a near death situation for the second time that day and it wasn't lunch time yet.

A sudden pressure came bearing down on my right calf as one of its limbs finally caught me. I fired the rest of my clip at the offending paw, causing it to flinch away, but dragging me along. A quick shake threw me out against the ground again and the voice in my head desperately demanded control again. I held back against it. I didn't know if my void abilities could hurt the thing, and the loss of control could mean becoming lunch in a very short amount of time.

Luckily, the Captain came to my rescue. He ran right up to it and chucked something into the open jaws. The beast stumbled for a moment in surprise and then attempted to spit out the package. Before if managed to clear it's throat there was a solid whump and the giant killer crashed to the ground, smoke pouring from its maw. The beast seemed to panic and leapt towards the underbrush, crashing its way through like a freight truck through aluminum.

I lay on my back, trying to catch my breath. My sides and leg hurt, but a quick manual check revealed nothing was bleeding. The captain's face filled my view as I lay there wheezing and he helped me get to a sitting position. His own uniform was torn in a couple places and his hat had been lost early in our encounter, leaving the small knit cap in plain view of the sunlight. I stared at the gaping hole in the foliage through which the creature had fled. "Thanks. Was that a grenade?"

"Smoke canister with double-stick tape on the outside. My Imam got me a set after I helped him out on a case"

I blew out a breath. "I've got to get me some of those."

He nodded matter of factly. "And a better gun, I know they recommend the 9-millimeter at the academy, but I'd never go on shift with anything less than a .38. Putting a hole in something doesn't always end it in our line of work."

I nodded. The wisdom of the statement had been clear. "That thing was smart. It acted like a person."

The captain inclined his head in agreement. "I bet it was the creature was what tore up the car. Now we know what it is, we are going to need more firepower. We'll double back to the car and radio to Chauncey."

I shakily got up and reloaded my pistol before holstering it. "I agree."

I was about halfway through my first day and now I had a missing person, a giant lizard-cat thing, and a potential gang assassination attempt on my life to worry about. Life in the agency was certainly not going to be dull.

Chapter 9

We drove to the city entrance in silence, too exhausted for more conversation. Mike verified with dispatch that Chauncey and Olivia had already arrived at the police headquarters. He then turned towards me. "Do you have a place in town?"

I gloomily gazed at the clock on the car dashboard with some regret. "Yes, but no key to get in. Was supposed to meet the landlady after orientation."

Mike shrugged his shoulders. "We have a couple cots up in the office we use for emergencies like this. Officially, you and Olivia will be on call for the night patrols who are watching the fence. Sleep in your uniform, because if that giant lizard-cat thing decides to attempt a breach you'll need to back them up. Chauncey and I will be heading up search teams who are going to check the woods for Frank Owens."

I couldn't help but look at him in surprise. "You are going out again? We barely survived our last encounter with that creature."

"We can't leave a man out there, especially not

a town citizen. The teams will be in big groups that will fall back rather than engage if the lizard-cat appears. If he's out there we should be able to find him."

I wanted to disagree, but tiredness and rank left little room to argue. Al-Radke dropped me off right in front of the Mhanke Heights Police station. The building was a squat red structure that appeared as solid as a brick and held the same aesthic. I let myself out of the car before turning back to the captain. "Sir - you mentioned you knew what happened to the second void-touched ever found. Were you a member of the team on that case?"

Mike Al-Radke gave me a slow nod and stared straight into my eyes. "It was my introduction to all this stuff. I'll never forget the sight of that crazy bastard hanging upside down from a rafter, chewing on the neck of her latest kill. That's what happens when void beings take control, they do things *their* way."

That stopped me. I couldn't think of a response. I just mutely nodded and closed the passenger side door behind me. It sounded impossible, but I had been living with a void predator in my head long enough to know it wouldn't even blink at doing something like that. In their world, everything was to be killed and you always ate what you killed. Without my mind to give it context, I could easily see the creature descending into cannibalism. Al-Radke left me there, thinking of the one statistic I'd never forget - there had been twenty known incidents of void-touched people. Only five hadn't been put down immediately or in their first year.

Inside the first floor I found a chaotic bustle of activity as a dozen officers of the police department readied themselves to patrol the town's fence line or join the search parties. The fence patrols would be joined by volunteers from the town itself. Almost every American town around the coasts had a fence, a 6-foot metal construct which was supposed to keep out the majority of alien wildlife. As a coastal city, Mhanke heights had gotten one early and it was an impressive setup with two separate sets of chainlink fencing about a foot apart from each other. I wasn't certain the fence would keep our massive friend out, but at least the patrols should be able to report a breach if it occurred.

I pressed into the mob of police officers, angling towards the second-floor stairs. The second floor consisted of a ring of offices that stared down into the building center. The ERC office was along the west side of the building, a hastily repurposed room that had probably served as work cubicles before the last renovation. Dust hung on the front half of the room, where boxes of unneeded things piled up. It was clear the whole thing had been set up in a hurry and nobody had ever had the time to create a more permanent place of work. Mike and Chauncey had their own desks along the rear of the space and two other desks had been set up with computers and binders on them. A television and some kind of game console had been set up in another corner. To my surprise, a pair of cots and a second hand couch had been set up with blankets and a handheld radio sat on one of the cots along with Olivia's carryon bags. She was playing on the game console with her sister, but paused to give me a nod as I walked up. I couldn't see the game's screen and the sound was off, but I assumed it was some kind of two player game. I'd have to ask the senior officers sometime how the office had managed to get a game console allowed.

I murmured some greetings to the two women but made a direct beeline for the empty cot. I unholstered and locked my firearm, but didn't bother taking off my shoes before my head hit the pillow. I was out quickly to a troubled and restless sleep.

Chapter 10

In my dream, I was back in Detroit. I sat with my best friend Jake and the rest of our gang, hanging out in one of the many abandoned houses. The summer heat had cooled down slightly and I could hear laughter and boasting as someone passed around a half-empty vodka bottle. Jake turned and said something to me, but I couldn't make out his garbled words clearly. As I turned my head back towards the party, I realized a beautiful red corvette sat in the living room. My blood ran cold; this was not any red corvette, but the one car I could never forget.

The doors were shiny red of arterial blood and I felt myself pulled towards the vehicle. I put a hand on the cold metal of the door handle and the world around me seemed to explode before contracting into an empty street. Jake and I were alone now, sitting in the car and taking off down an empty street of an industrial district. Jake pawed through the glovebox as I caressed the steering wheel and pushed the gas pedal down, pushing us to the kind of speeds only a dumb teenager would think was a good idea. A sick sense of dread filled me as I realized I couldn't remove my foot from the gas pedal. I wanted to scream that we needed to stop, that we had to turn away, to do something to avoid the street corner I knew was coming. Jake only laughed and laughed, not looking up as the world in front of us suddenly split open, ripping like a tearing backdrop. I panicked, but to my great surprise and relief, we drove right through the hole and came out the other side, still on the street. I laughed like a maniac as I pushed the car sharply around corners and left the tires smoking in a scorched circle at the end of a cul de sac. Time seemed to stand still and for a moment I could revel in the feelings I'd had back then - the power, the freedom, the excitement of being young and unstoppable. Jake whooped as I narrowly avoided clipping a mailbox and we took off down the thoroughfare like demons in the night.

Jake looked over at me, grinning from ear to ear. "You know, for an ugly half-gringo, you drive almost decently."

The feeling of power turned to one of camaraderie and I put an arm on the car windowsill. "Don't give me that Mexican bullshit. Your family has been in America longer than mine."

He snorted. "Yeah, but we don't forget."

I slapped his shoulder. "Fuck that shit. When's the last time you had a taco that wasn't from a drive thru?"

He pointed up at the night sky. "That's an excellent point. We should drive to Tijuana."

I shook my head and kept grinning. "You were always talking about leaving, but you never actually go anywhere."

"What and leave you alone with my crew? You'd have them all in jail before I got to the border"

"Just remember that when you come back and I'm running things, Ok?"

Jake laughed again. It was a old joke between us. We had both known neither of us would ever be more than small time, but it never hurt to dream. I turned another corner at speed and I heard the laughing cut off. Jake's voice suddenly became grave. "We got a problem."

I glanced in the rear-view mirror nervously. "Cops?"

"No." Came the flat response and Jake turned towards me again. His eyes had been replaced with black orbs and his teeth with a double row of fangs. "It's you, Marcus. You're the problem."

He had a gun in his hands now, aimed right at my temple. "Jake..." I started.

He fired. The bullet entered my skull but there wasn't any pain, any noise. Instead the world exploded again and I was in the awful place from the tear. The Void. The void isn't the real vacuum and emptiness of our outer space, but was filled with an empty ether that collected in great spheres which stretched out forever. They hung like bloated corpses in a river, spinning lazily to physics I could neither comprehend nor experience.

Every was made of the void-stuff. Between the great spheres were other, smaller concentrations who swam between them like sharks in the ocean. They were the beings of the void, barely formed creatures that swam and hunted and were hunted in those impossible distances. I stared down and realized there was no ground, no up, no point of orientation. Movement was impossible because there was nothing to move against. I screamed as noticed the movement in my chest. Something, one of those things, was inside me. I screamed as its face pushed out from my midsection, a long serpentine snout and a double row of fangs that clacked and strained for me. We were trapped together, thrashing in the void, as our entangled form drifted away from the car and towards an eternity of suffering.

In the real world, my body shot straight up like a rocket, mouth still formed in a wordless scream. My heart thudded in my chest and for a terrible moment I thought I could see movement just below my ribcage. Unfocused, I fell out of the cot and glanced in temporary bewilderment at the office before I remembered where I was. I took a moment to breathe, feeling my lungs fill with real air for a moment. LittleBird and Olivia slept, but I no longer could. I had not had this particular nightmare in years and I felt a churning feeling in the back of my head as the very real creature from my nightmare slumbered on, waiting for something to catch its interest. I sighed and went looking for coffee. I wouldn't be sleeping any more tonight and I might as well study the case.

<u>Chapter 11</u>

Morning sent its first rays over the horizon a few hours later. I had checked in with the dispatchers, two officers who had been way too chipper for 3am, and found out nothing exciting had happened for either the search parties or the patrols. Even the beat cops had little to report as much of the criminal element had decided to lay low that night. Once satisfied there was nothing immediately requiring my presence, I had showered, eaten, and put on a spare uniform.

Olivia and LittleBird had gotten up about an hour after I had; Olivia informed me neither of them needed as much sleep as normal people. I guessed there were some perks to being what the media calls Golems - people with artificial bodies. I wandered back into the office and noticed the teenager was gone. I walked over to Olivia. "Did the kid go home?"

She shook her head grimly. "Missed our house move in appointment. I asked one of the patrolmen to take her to school."

I raised an eyebrow. "Aren't you worried it will

give her fellow students a bad first impression?"

Olivia chuckled. "I suspect she's going to ask the officer to drop her off a block away. Not a girl like LittleBird doesn't make a big impression on anyone she meets anyway."

I was about to ask Olivia how her sister ended up with such a bizarre name, but was interrupted when the Captain and Chauncey walked into the room. Our leader had been up most of the night, but the only way you could tell was the slight amount of stubble perking up around his chin. He pulled out an old whiteboard on wheels and turned it to our assembled crowd. On top of the board the captain had written the words 'Frank Owens MIA', 'Lizard-Cat Containment', and finally 'Officer Ambush'

He opened up to our miniature circle by waving his marker at the board. "I know it has been a hell of couple days, but we've already run out more time than we can normally allow for a missing person. To make matters worse, I just got the report one of the fence teams found a hole in the fence not too far from the docks. It was slashed open so our monster friend may have breached containment." He wrote 'May be in Mhanke' under 'Lizard-Cat Containment'.

I felt alarmed. "Shouldn't we be out there looking for it?"

Chauncey shook his head. "Holes in the fence are not unusual. Smugglers, teenagers looking to avoid adult supervision, even the occasional metal scrapper all take a bite out of it on occasion. The hole may have been made by our gang members, looking to avoid notice. No one has seen the beast, and something that big is hard to miss on a city street. The creature could be holed up in a warehouse, though. It's a low point in the shipping season, so I bet at least one of them are empty." The captain added 'Empty Buildings' under the 'may be in Mhanke' comment.

"We will check on things once we figure out what we need to check. Running off half-cocked won't achieve anything. Let's start with the obvious, what do we know about the beast?"

Olivia piped up. "It killed one of the first two people it encountered but it doesn't seem to have done so to the other. Could it be smart? Taken a hostage?"

Chauncey took up the train of thought. "It did execute an ambush. It's clearly not afraid of humans, but executed a retreat when it was losing. Think it might be smart enough to keep Frank Owens as a bargaining chip?"

I shook my head. "I don't think it took a hostage. It didn't have Frank Owens with it when it attacked and I can't see those ginsu-knife claws being able to tie a rope. Assuming he didn't escape somehow, likely it snapped his neck and stashed him someone to eat later. Like a leopard stashing a kill."

Olivia made a face. "That is kind of pessimistic."

"It's smart, but all the behavior we've seen so far is normal for an alpha predator. In context, it is more likely to be interested in hunting and defending territory than a complex concept like negotiation."

Olivia didn't want to let it go. "Are you an expert on exoreality predators? "

I lowered my sunglasses to remind her I did have personal experience in the subject, but she only cocked a sarcastic eyebrow at me. Captain Al-Radke interrupted our face-making. "ExoReality creatures often follow traditional models but not always. It's safe to assume we are dealing with a clever predator until we have evidence otherwise. If it does have Owens as a hostage than it'll have to find a way to communicate his situation to us - hostages are useless if nobody knows you have them."

The captain pointed at final heading on the board, 'Officer Ambush'. "I'm most concerned about this. Nobody should have known you two were out there. Someone found out and brought enough firepower that they felt comfortable trying to take on 2 members of the ExoReality Containment agency and a pair of reservists in an open firefight. To make matters worse, unless they are camping out in the deep spaces between here and Riverbridge they are very likely back in town."

I was more in my element here. Gang studies had been my major at the academy. I listed off what I knew. "The suspects used mostly small arms and wore a mix of denim and leather - so it's safe to assume this is a biker gang. Probably a convoy-based group."

Chauncey nodded. "We get a lot of biker chapters that travel as escorts to the convoys. Some are blatantly gangs, but we can't do anything about it unless they commit a crime we know about. Could it have been a bandit gang? One of those nomadic groups that pick off lone travelers?"

I shook my head. "I don't think so. When a gang attacks a target, it's a risk-reward proposition. Looting a lone car is one thing, but you don't go attacking police officers unless you know the target is worth it. They lost 5 people in that attack. You don't do that over a couple wallets and a wedding dress. Did they have any tattoos in common?"

Olivia cocked her head for a moment and then recovered. "I forgot you can't see those things. They all had blood vein tattoos. All over their arms and their chests."

I froze and cursed myself for not asking the question when we'd been at the scene. "Were their vein tattoos over their older ones? Like they'd had one set but had written over them with the fresh tattoos?"

Chauncey turned his head to stare at me a moment. "Yeah they did. Made it hard to make out the orginal ones. Usually a red or black color"

"Damn." The word escaped my lips as pieces started to click into place.

The Captain had written the information about the tattoos onto the board, "Marcus? Can you ID the gang? I'm told it was your academy specialty."

I swallowed and nodded. "It's an Ardetha coven. They cover over their previous tats with the veins to show their commitment."

Chauncey and Captain Al-Radke froze in place, giving each other worried expressions. Olivia looked confused. "What the hell is an Ardetha coven?"

I cleared my throat and tried to collect my thoughts, trying to decide whether to tell her what was in the textbooks or what I had been told when living on the streets of Detroit. Pulling a breath in, I opted for the more 'official' version. "So the rifts have brought magic, monsters, and all the other alien junk we deal with in the agency, right? The one thing that we don't largely see is the old mythological beasts like werewolves, ghouls or vampires."

Olivia interrupted. "That makes sense. The rifts weren't around when people made those legends. I don't see how this relates to the topic."

Chauncey sat on a corner of his desk and answered her. "The connection is doctor Obadiah Partridge. He's a former geneticist who went off the deep end of mad science and now goes by the name Dr. Immortal. Total mad science whackjob. He apparently felt slighted that vampires weren't real and went about using rift based technologies to make them a real thing. He created Ardetha."

That got Olivia's attention. "Is it a drug?"

I waggeled my hand back and forth. "More like a series of genetic treatments delivered in a drug cocktail. Users sign up to get a permanent vampire-like experience over a few weeks of treatments."

The Captain picked up a marker and started filling out the most important details on the whiteboard. "The most important thing for law enforcement is that Dr. Partridge has been on the run for years and he's been using Ardetha subjects as test subjects to perfect his formula. The oldest generations had fangs and a tendency to have random heart attacks. The newer ones have enhanced strength, metabolism, an aversion to light, and a major aggression problem."

I picked up a pen off Olivia's desk and twirled it between my fingers as I filled out what wasn't in the text books. "Ardetha covens often recruit from smaller gangs who want the power. Those gangs form new covens that often recruit from middle and upper class youth who have romanticized the vampire myth. Once they are firmly embedded, they'll move on to another town. The original gang is often on the hook with the doctor to get newer treatments with fewer side effects. The new recruits can't ever go back to their former lives so turnover rates are low outside of violent death."

Olivia cocked her head and glanced at the board. "Why can't they go back?"

I missed a beat and dropped the pen. "For starters, its part of the gang ethos. It's why they cover up the old tattoos. More importantly, the upturned aggression and strength makes them volatile killers. You can't have a sit-down meal with an Ardetha user. Someone says the wrong thing and they are likely to murder the entire room. Generally, their lives only end in a lot of blood and violence."

Olivia sat down and turned on her computer. "Could the car contain something they wanted? Like narcotics or Ardetha treatments?"

Chauncey mused. "Possibly. The gangs know that anything they bring in is liable to search, so sometimes they hire a local to smuggle stuff in for them. If Owens was carrying a cargo, that would explain the ambush. They wouldn't want to lose the value of the stash or risk an investigation into who it was meant for."

Mike pointed his dry erase marker at me. "Anything else we know about these groups?"

I sighed. "Chauncey has the right of it. They look like a normal gang on the surface, but the changes knit them together tighter than normal. Nobody else will trust them, so they become very interdependent. Most gangs are either true believers trying to found the 'vampire race' or junkies working their way to affording a second set of treatments that are supposed to fix whatever is wrong with the one they got last. Odds are the core members were inducted at the same time, so they'll likely all have the same changes. Newer members will have a range of differences depending on when they were recruited. The fangs are usually a dead giveaway, so at least they'll be easy to spot. The fangs are a cosmetic change, but all the Ardetha treatments give them."

The captain updated the board. "Well that's more than we knew before. Ardetha gangs are under our purvey so we'll have to deal with them no matter what. Here's the major question. Who is Frank Owens and is he related to either of our other problems?"

Olivia read through the notes she and I had

compiled from police records, "He's a traveling businessman. Spends 3 days a week in the city and the rest in Mhanke Heights. Calls to relatives stated that they all attended a wedding last week and he was supposed to be on his honeymoon. It was his bride that was the other victim. No known priors for smuggling, although he has an assault charge for a fist fight a couple years ago."

I continued, glancing at an invisible list I was keeping in my mind. "So, if he is a smuggler, he was never caught. I checked with Crime Scene Investigation and the car is clean so far, but they are taking the panels out in case he was using a hidden compartment. His brand-new bride was a typist in the city, but she gave her resignation a few weeks ago."

"Anything else? Does he have any known contacts with the convoys?"

Olivia filled in for me. "Quite the opposite. He tended to travel alone. He apparently liked taking his chances to save time and money."

That had been brave, but stupid. A single mechanical failure could have left him traversing miles of countryside on foot, with no cell phone service outside of more than a couple miles from each city. The mobile phone companies had given up trying to maintain services out in the wilds. ERC and military vehicles did travel alone, but only with a satellite communicator or some thick armor plating. I mused. "We might be overthinking it. Frank might have been a customer that didn't pay or someone who had dirt on the gang. An ambush could have been meant to silence him."

Chauncey continued the thought. "It's also possible that it was a simple bandit raid. Ardetha gangs are notoriously aggressive. They might have simply been unable to stop themselves from attacking."

Captain Al-Radke finished adding our theories to the board. "We have an immediate problem - the Beast might be in town. Chauncey and I will head out to the docks once someone can rustle up the dock manager. There are only three warehouses, but it'll be a slow search. Olivia and Marcus, it had always been our plan for you two to partner under our oversight and we'll start that now. You are both fresh, so I want you to check out Frank Owens. He had an apartment along Sunset road. Get access to it and see if there is anything to connect him to the ambush or anything else relevant."

Chauncey grinned at me. "There's a second squad car in the parking lot. I'll let you fight it out over who drives." He tossed me a pair of beaten car keys.

Chapter 12

I got the joke once we got to the parking lot. The second squad car was clearly a hand-me-down from the police department. Someone, Chauncey I was guessing, had painted 'ERC' along the side in white paint. The car itself was an early 2000s model and had seen more than its fair share of dings and dents. I got into the driver's seat and grunted as I sat on half a radio that was spread out across the passenger's compartment. Olivia opened the driver side door and picked up the siren and lights controller, which was wired in but not mounted. She shoved it into the hole where the glove compartment should have been. I gave her a morose expression. "I'm thinking they didn't have much of a budget for a second car."

Olivia grunted. "Perhaps this is the ERC equivalent of hazing. Think there's a better car hidden somewhere else?"

I sighed and threw her the keys. "I doubt it. At least it runs."

She cocked her head and shook the key. "A man that doesn't want to drive?"

I sighed. "I can't see colors or lights. They weren't willing to give a driver license to someone who has to guess the state of traffic lights."

Olivia laughed and got into the driver seat. In a worrying start, the engine coughed but resumed operation as we took off from the parking lot.

Mhanke Heights wasn't a major town, and it only took about ten minutes to get to the apartment building. It was a newer construction, all painted concrete and cheap wood railings. A plaque on the outside proclaimed the building as the 'New Solar Apartment Complex'. We met the landlord in the entrance, who handed us a key and happily shuffled back to his apartment as soon as was polite. Climbing up the stairs, I was surprised to see that the stair railing appeared to be made of thin aluminum. It was bent in a couple places. Olivia gave the rickety railing a tap. "I have to wonder if that is legal. Don't put any weight on it."

Frank Owen's apartment was on the fifth floor, the very top of the building. Apparently, the builders hadn't heard of elevators. I silently thanked my physical conditioning instructors as I struggled to keep up with Olivia, who wasn't so much as winded. I huffed. "I have to ask, what kind of rift-changed are you?"

She referenced something on her phone as we started looking for the apartment. "Officially, I'm a Golem archetype."

I waved my hand over her. "Golem's a rather vast archetype. I've heard of fast healers and of being impervious, but you aren't like anything in the books at the academy."

"Officially, I'm one of a kind. Everything you see is a constructed facsimile," she poked at her arm, "it's not real flesh, but I manage a comparatively lifelike approximation. I can even bleed if I need to."

I glanced at her bare arms. They didn't appear any different than my own. "Officially?" I asked.

"I'm kind of an immigrant to here. The science boys think I came from the world known as the Eternal Planes, but I don't remember. My first memory is being taken out of my shipping container in New York City."

I glanced at the ceiling as I took that in, but it left me with more questions. I asked, "And your little sister, the one you rode into town with?"

Olivia flinched. "There is a more complicated story. Do me a favor and don't ask her about it. She and the others are self-conscious about it."

That earned a raised eyebrow. "There are more like her?"

Olivia smiled. "I have five more 'sisters', but they are all in college. How about yourself, any family?"

A wave of melancholy hit me. "I have a mother somewhere, I think. No one else. I - ah, left most of my past behind when I joined the academy."

That got a laugh. "Tall, dark, tanned, and without a past. You are really pushing that whole dark hero thing huh?"

I mocked looking offended. "You forgot handsome and witty"

She turned back to the task at hand. "When you demonstrate witty, I'll reconsider the sentence."

After all the drama of the past 24 hours it felt cleansing to banter. "You are just picking on me because I'm special."

Olivia stopped at a door halfway down the hall. "I wouldn't go that far. Tall, Dark men are a dime a dozen and most have better banter."

Ouch. That truth hurt. I made a shooing motion. "Open the door, officer. Some of us have detective-ing to do."

Olivia opened the door with a flourish, bowing to allow me into the apartment. I got a step in and stopped so quickly you would have thought I'd walked into a wall. Olivia pulled up short as well and we surveyed the scene. The modestly sized apartment was a wreck. I had thought that the spacious dining room window had been open, but in truth the window and much of its frame was simply gone. The couch had been partially embedded upside down into the far wall. Plaster was everywhere. The dinner table had been smashed to mere shards and a giant hole had been dug in the center of the living room. I put on my scene-handling gloves, but had trouble tearing my eyes away from destruction. There were deep gashes in the walls and the whole room looked like a hurricane had fought the Tasmanian devil to the death. It was horrible enough that Frank Owen's car and wife had been destroyed, but life wasn't done screwing him it seemed.

Olivia whistled as we entered. I felt like I was walking through a battlefield where someone's, Frank Owens', life had died an incredibly messy death. I examined the remains of the living room while Olivia tried unsuccessfully to dial the Captain, but only got his voicemail. I tried shifting through the remains of the coffee table and its former contents while she raised dispatch instead. I pulled out my phone and let it read me summaries of the mail. Most of the pieces of paper turned out to be bills, with a few wedding congratulations thrown in. I made a stack of the photos - it would be easier to have Olivia tell me what was in them than to wrestle useful information out of the phone app. I missed being able to simply see pictures and written words. The novelty of my changed sight had quickly soured the first time I'd picked up a restaurant menu.

Lacking any immediate success, I decided to

examine the hole in the floor. It had initially looked like more random damage, but closer examination revealed that an entire piece of crossbeam had been removed at some point in the past and a metal frame had been placed to form a kind of box. Looking up I realized that the hole would have been under the coffee table before it had been tossed. The smuggler theory was looking stronger. Feeling about, I could pick up a fine powder of some kind and a fair amount of vicious liquid in the corner. The liquid was too oily to be blood, so I called Olivia over.

She came around the corner of the tiny kitchen. "I can't raise the captain, but dispatch says they'll send the CSI guys and a couple beat officers over. Apparently, the warehouses screw with cell phone reception."

I waved at the hole. "It's a smuggler's box. A place to stash illicit items before handing them over. Can you run the test kit on the stuff around the rim? The tester doesn't have a 'blind mode'."

Olivia shrugged and put a finger down on the powder, then gave it a lick. My jaw dropped. "Are you nuts?"

She gave me a bland expression. "It's cocaine. I've tasted it before"

I spluttered. "You can't lick random powders! What if you end up buzzed on the job?"

That earned me a raised eyebrow. She pointed at her head. "No a real human brain remember? I could snort an entire package and it wouldn't bother me."

"Still not a wise idea, what if it was poison or something?"

"Still not going to affect me."

"Golem poison?"

She gave me a mocking smile and moved over to the corner with the liquid splash across it. "You made that up." Apparently, the taste test wasn't successful, because she actually pulled out her tester kit and took a sample. The tester kits were a common sight amongst both ERC and Narcotics officers. The kits contained the latest in computing advances and mana-tech to provide a handheld device and supplementary vials that could identify some hundred common narcotics. I knew from experience that the machines were perpetually out of date on synthetic drugs, but it should be able to identify the more run of the mill stuff. Olivia screwed a sample vial into the top of the device and studied the readout. After a while she peered over at the stain.

"It's a mixed compound containing human blood, a viscous fluid, metal bits and a tiny amount of heroin," she stated. "Can you tell if there's a mana charge?"

I nodded. "The charge is what drew my attention in the first place. Ardetha?"

She scrolled through the output. "The tester isn't helpful with complex mixes like this, but it sounds right. Blood for theme, a suspension compound to keep it stable, the mana-nanites to rewrite the DNA and a narcotic to reduce the pain and make it feel good."

"Our beast breaks in through the window and takes the drugs? How would it know where to find them? For that matter, why would it want them in the first place?"

Olivia gazed at me smugly. "The lizard-cat might be smarter than certain law officers thought. It could have interrogated Frank Owens for the location."

"So it could, what? Snort coke and try to get more fangs? Ardetha is useless if you aren't a baseline human. Most rift-changed can't be dosed without dying horribly."

"Perhaps it's collecting bargaining chips? Frank's well-being to keep us in check? Drugs to keep the gang in check?"

I sighed. "The captain was right, if it was seeking to negotiate it would try to communicate. Besides, there's nothing in the city it could want that it couldn't get hunting out in the wilds."

Olivia went over to the stack of pictures. "Well at least this confirms the link between Frank Owens and the gang. You want to know another weird thing?"

I scratched my head. "Is it possible for this to get any weirder?"

She picked up the pictures and brought them close to her face, one at a time. "Someone ripped or scratched out Frank Owens in all these pictures. Friends, his bride, family all left alone but somebody went through each of these photos and scratched him out."

I put out a hand and felt the surface of a photo, I hadn't noticed it at the time, but it was rough where someone had used a knife or similar instrument to scrape out the rough shape of a man. "The beast couldn't have done that. Claws are way too massive for something this delicate."

I tapped on the photo. Had someone arrived after the beast? Had the beast had had someone with it? And who had the drugs? This case was getting complicated fast, and each answer was only generating more questions.

I pondered and rubbed the photo. "This beast doesn't only know Frank Owens. I think it hates him, but I cannot for the life of me understand why."

Olivia sighed. "Let's get CSI in here. We need

an answer to that question if we are going to figure out where this thing is going to go next"

Chapter 13

I got a call from Chauncey while waiting for CSI to start processing the scene. His voice was the calm professionalism of a veteran officer, but there was a breathlessness to his voice. "First things first," he said, "did you find anything at the apartment?"

I thought it was odd that Chauncey was the one making the call, but he was a senior officer on the case. I filled him in on what we had found. His voice changed into a frustrated, but controlled tone. "That doesn't seem possible. Did anyone hear the beast enter or leave?"

"No, but the flanking apartments are empty. There's only a couple people on this floor."

"Any idea when the break-in occurred?"

I went over my mental notes. "There was a patrol through here around 4 am. I don't know if they didn't see the damage or it hadn't happened yet."

Chauncey cursed. "The break in the fence happened around 6:00 am. That thing is the size of a small car. There's no way it could have traveled from the fence to the apartment and back to the docks without someone seeing it."

The comment piqued my interest. "There was evidence of it at the docks?"

"Yeah." There was a pause as Chauncey collected himself. "It was here when we spooked it out from some unused pallet stacks. Charles Greeson - you probably didn't know him, but he's an excellent cop - he had to be shipped off to the emergency room with half his left arm gone. Two other officers have minor wounds.". He paused again, as if uncertain if he should continue. "Mike got bit in the shoulder and right arm distracting the beast from Greeson. He's going to be ok, but he's headed for the emergency room as well. The docs will let us know his condition as soon as they are able."

I sucked in my breath and Olivia noticed my reaction. "You'll gives us a call when the hospital lets you know the captain's condition?"

"I will. In the meantime, I'm going to go over local business cameras and see if I can figure out how this thing is getting around without being seen. I want you and Olivia to follow up on the drugs angle. I'm going to text you..." There was awkward pause. "Can you read text messages?"

I sighed internally and reminded myself it

wasn't his fault that he'd never dealt with someone with my condition before. "My phone can read it to me," I stated. "Olivia can help me out too if you want to send a picture."

"Good enough. I'm going to send you a couple case files you can access at headquarters. Look up a guy called Colgate. He's a regular dealer in this town and will always know more than most if someone is selling drugs on his turf. Get the files and meet me at Park and Main in 3 hours. I have an idea for how we can get our friend to help us out."

"3 hours? It won't take us that long to get the files."

Chauncey chuckled. "God, I love the enthusiasm. It'll take me three hours to review the camera footage and get over there. If you want something to do in the meantime, try seeing your landlady. Dispatch tells me she's looking for you. I bet Olivia is in a similar boat."

I winced. I'd completely forgotten to reschedule the meeting to sign the final paperwork and get the keys. I let Chauncey go and informed Olivia of the situation. I felt a little relieved when she winced as well at the mention of landlords. "I knew I forgot something. Convoy was supposed to deliver our things today to the moving company."

I smirked. "You'll just have to tell them the city needed you desperately."

Olivia paused and spoke is a sarcastic voice. "I'm sorry I'm late, there's a giant cat-tree-lizard loose in the town. It's killing people, but don't panic - it might only be ingesting a few kilograms of street grade cocaine."

I rolled my eyes and hoped Chauncey's lead would produce something. We needed something before things escalated again.

Chapter 14

After we got back to the headquarters I elected to walk to the rental home on my own, letting Olivia take the squad car to her own residence. Earlier in the month I had found a decently sized home that flanked the original downtown area and dated back to when Mhanke Heights had a population only a quarter of what it was now. It was a two-bedroom home with just enough yard not to be directly butting against the street and a tiny backyard too small to justify anything but grass. The house was miniature by Mhanke Heights standards, but the location right behind the stores and offices of the original downtown meant I was paying more rent than Olivia for half the space. Like anyone whose disability precluded their ability to drive themselves anywhere, I had been willing to pay a premium to be within walking distance of a grocery stores and general shopping. As I walked to my new home, I took a moment to contemplate what I was doing.

Pay with the agency was substantial compared to a lot of blue color work, but part of me still couldn't believe I could afford the place. I had spent most of my youth in a succession of the type of 'hotels' in which residents pay weekly and the landlord brings a couple things around any time he has to collect the rent. Then there had been 5 of us living in a space less than 600 square feet. My brothers and I slept in the living room at night and my sisters slept with my mother. Now I was looking at almost twice that space for only myself.

The house appeared to be as promised, with a tiny pair of windows in front and some old school wooden sidings. There was even a modest porch that could hold a chair and possibly a potted plant or two. Not that I had any clue how to raise plants.

A short, elderly woman stood on the sidewalk in front of the house. Assuming she was the landlady, I offered her my hand. "Hello ma'am. I'm Marcus Black, are you Henrietta Sharpton?"

The woman appraised my uniform and smiled in a lightly embarrassed manner. "Officer Black, I'm glad to meet you. Let's take a look inside, shall we? I'd hate to keep you away from work."

She had almost gotten me to the door, before I realized I was been ushered inside before I could examine the outside of the property. I fished about for the cause. "Mrs. Sharpton? Does that sign say what I think it does?"

My neighbor had a sign up in his yard. One of those arm-sized, pasteboard numbers used for yard sales and kid's birthday parties. I squinted at it. The tall glued-on letters were barely visible to my site, but I got the gist. There were three posterboard letters covering the sign. I. W. P.

Damnit.

I didn't need to be told the implication. The jerk wanted the whole neighborhood to know an Innate Weaponized Person had moved in. I couldn't have gotten a worse case of bad press if the sign had read 'convicted felon' or 'serial killer' on the sign.

Mrs. Sharpton was clearly embarrassed. "I'm so sorry. Mr. Bain has strong opinions. I asked him to remove it."

I sighed. "It's ok. He has the right."

That was sadly true. IWP was the official government designation for the more dangerous rift-changed like me and there wasn't anything illegal about pointing it out. We weren't a protected minority or covered under any government laws - technically the opposite. We weren't banned from anything officially, but if someone put up a 'No Innate Weaponized Personnel' sign it wasn't legally clear if that was enforceable or not. I was still of the opinion that the whole thing was an excellent example of the government doing something halfway and being surprised when their solution made things worse. My other half didn't really understand the concept, but it growled at the idea of someone challenging us. Wonderful. I'd be the middleman between two beings who were destined to hate each other but be unable to talk directly.

I realized I was making a face and settled it back to the pleasant one reserved for people you somewhat like and are in business with. "You said in your email that there was a back patio? Can I see it?"

Mrs. Sharpton was glad to leave the subject of the sign behind and escorted me in. The rest of the tour was better. There was a broken step and a couple wall sockets that didn't work, but the structure was well-built and I couldn't find a cockroach anywhere despite looking very thoroughly. Hey, you grow up in certain places and you learn what really matters in a living space. We were looking at the bedroom when I realized what had been tickling the back of my mind. "Mrs. Sharpton? The agreement didn't specify that this was a pre-furnished rental. Why is there a bed here?"

Henrietta flushed a little. "It was left behind by the previous occupant. I wasn't strong enough to move it. I know you came across country, so I was hoping you could use the thing. It's all been cleaned."

I winced. "The previous occupant is dead, aren't they?"

She hedged "Not dead... they fell into a rift and... never came out."

"I'm guessing the rift was on this property?"

The rental agreement bent slightly as she clutched it to her chest. "It's gone now. I was hoping you wouldn't worry about it."

It was a fair point; rifts were my job. "You've got me there. Don't worry ma'am. The house is perfect for my needs. I'll have to get to work soon so let's sign those papers."

Mrs. Sharpton was clearly relieved as I signed the paperwork. I hadn't thought about it when we had arranged the rental, but the recent death and rift event had probably driven the price down. Likely she had been overjoyed that I'd been willing to rent the place at all. I hoped Olivia had a better time with her place.

Chapter 15

Half an hour later, I had unpacked my entire duffel bag and was standing on the sidewalk when I saw Olivia come up with the squad car. I opened the passenger side door and grumbled as I peered in the back seat. "Is that a fruit basket?"

She grinned up at me. "And baked goods. My neighbors were happy to have a cop in the neighborhood."

Her vision slid over my shoulder, noticing the sign on my neighbor's yard. "I'm guessing you didn't have as warm of a reception."

"I haven't technically met my neighbors yet. Possibly, they are as excited to have a potential danger in their neighborhood as yours is to have an officer of the law."

She winced, but I held up a hand to forestall any more conversation on the subject. "Let's head over to where Chauncey wants us. Apparently, this is a backup location for our dealer and Chauncey has made some arrangements to help us out."

A few minutes later I was looking at Fredrick

Trotsky, AKA 'Colgate' from across a dingy street corner. Chauncey had given us a basic rundown on the kid and the gang he worked with. It was a setup I knew well - an older male convinces kids to sell narcotics for him at known locations while staying safe from direct arrest by not participating in the sales himself. The gimmick here was that the gang had gotten ahold of a teleport spell of some kind and would whisk the evidence away before the inventory could be seized. The local police detectives had been trying varying schemes to foil this problem, but Chauncey was a specialist in spellcraft and said he could handle the problem. Chauncey blithely strolled over to 'Colgate's usual spot, sending the kid scurrying to the parking lot entrance I now watched him at, a backup location his customers would know about. He lounged in front of a city trash can and played on his phone. My part of the plan was simple, I simply waited until he was calm and settled and then openly walked across the road towards him, uniform and badge clearly visible for all to see. Colgate stiffened and his hands moved behind him, no doubt shifting the package containing his narcotics around. He tried to look nonchalant as his back leaned against the lid of the trash can. I saw the flick of the lid move as he shoved his fanny pack inside. Instead of trying to stop him, I leaned up against the nearby brickwork and tried to give an appearance of nonchalance as he did. I'm certain our mutual faking of the mood only made it more awkward.

"Fredrick Trotsky? You're under arrest for narcotics dealing."

His mouth turned into a thin line of triumph as he displayed empty hands. "What narcotics? I've got nothing."

I nodded my head at the approaching police cruiser. Chauncey drove up like a triumphant general and opened his door with a flourish. His passenger, one Detective Williams, happily stepped out and raised a battered and dirty fanny pack.

Colgate's eyes bugged out of his head at the sight of his stash. I smiled grimly as he realized that something had gone terribly wrong and tried to take off down the street. Olivia stepped out of the Happy Flowers shop she had been standing in and the poor kid bounced right off of her as he failed to duck around her. Olivia didn't even slow down as she rolled him onto his back and cuffed him. I grinned like a kid in a candy store. After nearly two days of chasing and being chased, actually being part of an arrest made me feel much better. Even if it was a non-agency arrest.

Detective Williams was smiling even larger than I was as we leaned Colgate up against the car. "I got to tell you, this disappearing thing you do with the package? It was pretty neat trick. Thing is, my friend Chauncey here was able to read those runes and make some modifications. He reached back and held up a box. "He updated a bunch of them to respond to this beacon he inked on the bottom of my evidence collection box. I bet it'll be rather full by day's end."

Colgate turned pale and said nothing.

Williams struck a conciliatory tone. "Now I know 2 things. One; that you guys were so confident in this teleport-thing that you've probably been failing to keep fingerprints off the packages, including Mr. DeMarco. Two; that Mr. DeMarco's suppliers are going to expect their money irregardless of whether or not the product was sold."

Williams continued, acting as if Colgate had just won some tremendous prize. "You however, are in luck. You're my first catch so I'm going to offer you a deal. Answer some questions for my friends, write out a statement detailing your relationship with DeMarco, and you'll get our cooperative witness package."

A glimmer of hope danced in the teenager's eyes. "You'll let me go?"

Williams shook his head in mock sadness. "No, but reduced jail times, better prison assignment, possibly not throwing you into the same cell as everyone else I'm picking up today. "

Colgate bit his lip but nodded his head. "I'll spill, but you keep Bossman off me, right?"

Chauncey chortled. "'Bossman' is going to have his hands too full to worry about you if you help. Let's start with some easy questions. Did you know Frank Owens?"

Colgate's eye shifted around. "Maybe."

"He had a stash of cocaine and Ardetha in his apartment. That ring any bells?"

Colgate looked confused for a moment. He murmured. "But he stopped taking jobs from..." I saw a light dawn in his eyes. "Shit. He's working for the new guys."

Now we were getting somewhere. Chauncey picked up on the thread. "The 'new guys'?"

The kid was more than willing to let the conversation drift in this direction, away from his friends and boss. "You want to know about the coven. Burnlight, burning light, something like that. "

"Sure kid. What are they selling? ManaDrunk? Methamphetamines?"

"Nah, it's cheap stuff. Pixie, Green, Party Poppers, perhaps some Juice."

Cocaine. Marijuana. MDMA. Heroin. It was quite the array of product, but the kind of things a gang might first sell to raise some cash and get a feeling for the market. Once the gang settled and had some loyal customers they'd branch out into more profitable stuff. They'd need Frank Owens to get the drugs in, since he wasn't searched and they'd need people to sell the stuff on the street. Only the truly desperate would buy their drugs knowingly from an Ardetha user. I cleared my throat. "Colgate. Who's running for them? Who's making the sales?"

He shrugged. "Bunch of kids the Bossman didn't want. He chose us instead, so they had to work with the new guys. A couple of rich kids on the payment plan."

I nodded. "Teenagers like you, plus a couple people that want to join. Do you know any of them personally?"

"Hell no. Bossman would have killed me if I'd been talking to one of those losers. They are all on the payment plan, you know? Getting fangs if they sell enough shit. At least Bossman is looking out for us you know?"

Taking care of you. That was how the senior gangers always put it. Nevermind that half the profits went for their own drug habits or to buy things they wanted. Nevermind that they'd leave you to rot if you got caught. The senior members would always tell you how important and protected you were, all lies revealed the moment you were a liability. My teeth ground together a bit as I debated giving my opinion on how little 'Bossman' was worth, but it didn't matter. This kid was headed to prison, conceivably a rehab center if he was lucky. With any luck, Mike DeMarco would spend a decade or two behind bars. "You know where they are set up? Where we can reach the dealers?"

Colgate gave me a weaselly grin. "The dealers don't have spots, but I know where the gang hangs out. The Last Line. They've been there for days. Chased a friend of mine right out of there. "

As if on cue, there was a flash and a thunking sound in WIlliam's evidence box. He reached in and examined a scuffed handbag. "It would appear my partner is getting started. I got to get this guy downtown if he wants to start writing that confession." He turned to the young dealer and guided him to the car's back seat. "Just think 'Minimum Security', Colgate, and don't leave any details out."

Chauncey turned back to us. "I've gone over the cameras and still can't explain how our 500-pound lizard is getting around town. I'm going to drop these two off and check in with the captain. Grab lunch and get back to headquarters to enter your case notes. The Last Line doesn't open until sundown at 7pm, so it might be the only chance you get to do so."

Chapter 16

The alley led out onto the town's main street, so Olivia and I stopped at a restaurant called "Salazar's Choice" and picked up a couple hamburgers to go. I was relieved to see that not only did Olivia eat, but apparently quite well given the two half pound burgers she had consumed. I would have loved one of the half-pounders, but the exercise to burn it off wouldn't have been worth it. I tried not to mope was I ordered my slightly-healthier normal sized cheeseburger. We walked across the street to the Headquarters to greet the tired but resolute office staff downstairs. Half the staff was sleeping in cots spread between the desks, while the other half manned radios or worked on computers. Though the emergency had temporarily been rescinded for the beat officers, it was clear the office staff was still pulling double-shifts to document and manage the after-effects.

Olivia nudged me as we climbed the stairs. "Remind me to get those guys donuts or something. They look worse off than we do."

I nodded and opened the door to the ExoReality Containment office. Chauncey was already gone, a note on the door simply stated 'Mike stable. Discharge later tonight. Contact me via cell.'

That was excellent news. If the captain was in and out in a day, then it must have only been a flesh wound. I suspect that he and Chauncey would already be working the case from the hospital room. Olivia examined the two desks with their untouched computers. "Do you have a preference?"

I shrugged, tapping my sunglasses. "It doesn't matter. I can't use either one."

"How are you going to fill out reports?"

"I'll record it in audio. Its possible my friend Chris from the academy knows where I can pick up a dictation program or something."

Olivia chose the desk closest to the gaming console, and I walked over to the one nearest the glass wall. I hadn't owned anything before I entered the academy, so my sole contribution to claiming the desk was to slide my pistol into the offered mag-holster bolted to the underside. That was a nifty feature.

Olivia on the other hand was unpacking way more equipment than could ever be held in a desk: Various pieces of mana-tech, spare evidence collecting gear, even an honest to god chemistry kit was spread all throughout the area as she tried to get it all to fit on or in the desk. I tried to look busy arranging a pen I found in the top drawer.

Finally, we settled into actually getting into the reports. The sound of Olivia's typing and my quiet talking into the phone filled the office. After a while I got bored and checked out what Olivia was doing. It's hard for me to make out all the details of a person, but I could see enough to tell me a bit about her. Her hair was packed close to her head in those tight curls and the bandage on the side of her head had been removed. Her uniform was still somehow well-fitted and in place, despite all the running around we had done today. Everything about her seemed to be extremely well organized and in control. It must have contrasted heavily with my perpetually disheveled appearance. Thinking on the contrasts between us, I couldn't help but ask, "Olivia? You mind if I ask you something personal?"

She glanced over from her screen. "I wondered when Q&A would start. Seems like people always have a thousand questions about what I am."

"Trust me, I know the feeling. You don't have to answer if you don't want to."

She smiled, crinkling up her nose. "Question for Question? Pass if you don't want to answer?"

That was more than I had meant to commit to, but it was fair. I nodded. "Sure. In that case go first."

She peered directly at me then, cocking her head like always. It reminded me of a curious owl. "Why join the ERC? I know most IWPs do, but why you?"

I contemplated on how much of that I wanted to answer. "Most IWPs join because you basically get the credits for it during the two years of IWP'safety' training. Means only two more years to a career. That was true, but I ..." I paused for a moment. "I wanted to make up for something in my past, do some good for others. My turn. Pass if you want to, but if you are a construct, why a woman? Why an African one?"

She laughed. "Most people are too shy to ask. Believe it or not, but I came out of the box this way. I'm not actually African - I'm not certain why I look like one. I'm guessing I was built to resemble my creators."

I ran a finger over my badge. "Does that get weird?"

"Hey! It's my turn!" she chided. "What's it like having someone else in your head?"

"'It is dormant most of the time. Like being asleep, but mostly it's because he doesn't care about what's going on outside of violence or food. My other half is a baby by their kind's standards so he only really communicates via emotions and shoving his willpower at me. The more mature ones can talk, and mature void-touched like Victor claim they've ceased being separate beings, thinking in concert and without conflict."

"It sounds like a awfully exhausting experience. "

"And for not much benefit, being void-touched can help mitigate the danger from bullets or make me dangerous in a brawl, but all of those abilities pale to a good service-issued pistol. There's the eyesight, but it's little more than what a decent off the shelf mana-scanner could do, not counting the creepy soul-sight bit. Back to my question, is it weird being seen as black? I mean this is America - there's a lot of baggage with that."

Olivia stopped typing and touched the curls of her hair. "It was at first, but it's a positive community to be a part of. Africans know what it's like to be looked at suspiciously for walking down the street and I can relate. Most African people are little put off by the fact that I'm not human at first, but there's a shared experience there."

I raised an eyebrow. "The shared experience of being judged silently by white strangers?"

She gave a short bark of a laugh. "You'd be surprised."

Given my own pale skin, I couldn't easily relate. I added it to those things I'll never understand but have to accept. Like having English as a second language, or breasts. All mysteries I'll never experience personally. Olivia started arranging beakers on her desk, having apparently hit the limit of how long she could sit still. "You've mentioned your mentor's name was Victor. Was that Victor Ward?"

I leaned back. "Yeah. He was kind of my mentor in the program. All the Void-touched and Forsaken archetypes get assigned a mentor when they enter the IWP program. Void-touched are extremely rare, so There's only about three guys who could have mentored me."

She glanced up at the ceiling and mused. "So, you know Static, have you met Glitch?"

I could hear Victor's pained sigh in my head. Victor Ward and Atticus Mason were two of the original five officers who had formed the FBI predecessor unit that had handled things before the ERC was created. Victor was a void-touched like me and Atticus was a shifter, a rift-changed which could bend their location in space time to play havoc with the laws of inertia and momentum. Their codenames in the unit had been 'Static' for Victor and 'Glitch' for Atticus. Thanks to media coverage, people had a bad habit of using their codenames instead of their real names. As if they were super heroes and not a pair of grumpy veteran detectives. "I've met them both, as well as Casey - the original FBI agent that formed the unit. They are relatively normal people so long as no one is shooting at them."

"Have you seen someone shoot at them?"

"No, but that is another question isn't it?"

Olivia made a shooing motion. "Do you have a question?"

"If you are a construct like you say, how do you have 6 sisters? LittleBird clearly isn't the same kind of construct you are."

Olivia's face darkened, and a cloud passed over her features. "Pass."

I recognized the warning signs and made a placating motion. "Fair enough. I've got a few things I don't tell just anyone as well."

She didn't answer me directly. Instead she pointed up at the clock. "It's getting close to 7:00. We should check out the bar once it starts to fill up."

Well damn. I hadn't meant to kill the mood. That's always the problem - you never know where people's hurts are. They are like hidden landmines that you can't avoid, only mentally mark them as places to avoid after you trigger them. Still, she was a professional and I knew I could rely on that.

<u>Chapter 17</u>

We arrived at The Last Line Bar and Grill roughly 15 minutes after it opened, parking the beat-up squad car as close to the road as we could. It had clearly been a Country-themed restaurant at some point in its youth, and the inside was a goofy mix of old school wooden fixtures and plastic 50s style diner tables. The owner had clearly not spent much on décor. A bar of sorts was against one wall, with a series of dining tables along the other. A pair of pool tables dominated the space between them. A gaggle of Convoy workers and truck drivers sat against the bar, while a pair of the dining tables and the nearby pool table was taken up by a half-dozen toughs. All of whom had the vein tattoos of Ardetha gang members. I chose my target, a squirrely guy sitting only a little apart from the others at the bar and motioned for Olivia to follow me.

The entire population of the bar had tensed up when we had entered, but all the regulars relaxed once we made our way towards the gang members. I made a mental note that this bar probably had more than a passing familiarity with people avoiding law enforcement. The men at the pool table noticed us, but didn't make any moves as I sidled up next to the older man. He was a slightly spastic example of an early Ardetha user, nervously flinching as he moved like some kind of methamphetamine fueled squirrel. He probably had the twitch from the less effective nerve treatments and needed an update badly to shake the side effects. Each Ardetha gang had a couple guys like this, shifted around between covens as a reminder that someone else had it worse than you and desperately trying to make good long enough to get a less destructive treatment than they had gotten. Most would never get it, as there was no need to do favors for someone so desperate and with nowhere else to go.

The Squirrel glanced over at me nervously but said nothing. Since I hadn't actually entered their space, none of them would want to start anything until I either opened my big mouth or crossed that invisible line. I chose to open my big mouth.

"You strike me as someone who needs some help relaxing, friend. What are you drinking?"

The Squirrel glanced fearfully over at his companions and mumbled a feeble brushoff.

I brushed the words off and barged on ahead. "Pity. I stopped drinking myself a few years ago. Not allowed since I got the patch, you know?"

His eyes bulged as he eyes glanced at the IWP patch on my shoulder. Good. He didn't know I barely qualified as an Innate Weaponized person and there was no reason not to let him assume I wasn't a massive danger to him and his friends. I smiled at him as if he was an old friend that hadn't seen each other in a long time. "Now buddy, I think we might be getting off on the wrong foot. What's your name?"

He stammered a little, his condition and nervousness making his jaw tremble. "G... George. J. Just George."

I put an arm around him. "Wonderful to meet you, George. Now, I want to see if you know a mutual friend of ours. Does Frank Owens ring a bell?"

I don't know if it was dropping the name or putting an arm around George that did it, but I felt the heavy weight of an extremely well-calloused hand fall on my elbow. A massive example of Cro-Magnon evolution had ambled up behind me, complete in a denim jacket which had more than a few washed out bloodstains on it. I noticed the Cro-Magnon's vein tattoos were newer, laid over a bunch of one percenter tattoos. "We don't know a Frank Owens. I think you should walk away."

Olivia glided up behind the brute and tapped him on the back. "Now, now, why don't you let them talk while you and I..."

He didn't let her finish. The brute turned and

swung a massive straight punch that probably could have dented steel. Olivia's body went flying like it had been hit by a truck, slamming her into a dining table. She didn't so much as flinch. Instead, she picked herself up like the dozen foot flight was a minor inconvenience. The incongruity of her seemingly 120-pound frame bouncing back from what had been a superhuman blow seemed to stymy the giant for a moment and the brute stood there and gaped.

Olivia wasn't stupid. She took a shuffling step forward and laid a solid kick right in his nuts. I swear the giant man lifted off the ground slightly. I don't care if you are a genetically modified super-brute, there's no shaking off a blow like that. He fell right over on his front, clutching his probably ruptured manhood.

That was when the room exploded into a brawl. Squirrel took a swing at me, but had trouble aiming the blow. I took it on the shoulder and knocked him off his perch. The little bastard scrambled away before I could cuff him. I glared at his backside as he scrambled into the bathroom. Damn. I turned towards the brawl. My partner was getting swarmed. Blows hammered down at Olivia, but she just bounced between them, giving out as much punishment as she was getting. They couldn't beat her, but she wasn't arresting anyone while getting thwacked around like a new gang initiate. She put another man onto his butt before I got there and I let my other half gain more control as I swept the legs out from another offender. With the Squirrel gone, we had only six of the gang members left. I didn't know how many we had started with, but we only needed to bring a one or two in. The rest could be allowed to run for it before we brought the full force of the law on them. I pulled another goon off my partner and she started getting the upper hand as space opened up.

I'm a decent fighter, I always have been. I probably could have outfought most of my class in a one on one match, but Olivia was a machine. Her technique lacked finesse, but she maximized her ability to take a punch. One poor bastard hit her across the head with a right hook, but she simply rolled with the blow and grabbed the offending limb, twisting it out of its socket. I dueled the latest goon I'd pulled off of her, but he was as fast as I was and could hit harder where his blows landed. I threw a swift kick at his legs, but he took it on the shin and replied with a jab towards my face. I ducked at the last moment, letting the blow skim my ear and returning a body blow that rocked the suspect back. A follow up blow dazed him, but the thug recovered quickly. I wasn't going to wear this target down, so I dodged another sweeping blow and closed to grapple. I got one hand behind his back, but Ardetha had made these guys incredibly strong. The void predator in me wasn't about to lose a wrestling match and we pressed against each other, his genetically altered strength versus my otherworldly enhanced muscles. I slipped the cuffs over one wrist and fought to get the other wrist in place. I gritted my teeth, trying to get the other wrist closer to the cuffs. Almost there...

I was inches from finishing the job when the bathroom exploded.

My opponent had been prepared for a lot, but not for an exploding bathroom. I took advantage of the distraction to finish cuffing the suspect. Despite the cuffs, he tried to run for it and it took me a moment to understand why. The bathroom hadn't just exploded. Something had exploded through the bathroom wall. A very familiar massive green shape sprang out of the rubble and dust. The Beast had come to the Last Line and it wasn't looking terribly friendly. I cursed and pushed my suspect behind me. One of the gang members tried to run for the door, but the movement only attracted the beast's attention. It sprang on the unlucky man and bit him in half. Jesus. I fumbled for my sidearm and braced myself. The deep-set eyes on the thing rolled over to where I was and a deep rumbling growl issued from its throat. I froze as its head followed the eye's direction slowly and the whole animal turned to face me directly.

I raised my firearm. "Nice Murder-Kitty. Want to answer a few questions?"

It roared what was probably the lizard-feline equivalent of a no. I responded by squeezing the trigger on my pistol and putting as many shots as I could towards the mouth of the thing. I think I might have chipped a tooth. Possibly knocked off some plaque. In response, the massive beast charged. I don't care what superpowers you have, if something the size of a rhinoceros charges towards you, you get out of the way. I dodged to the left and rolled over a chair. The scene was bedlam. The gang members had no illusions about what the greatest threat was. A shotgun and several pistols fired at the animal, but most of it only bounced off the creature's hide. Olivia held her ground and waited for the last moment, unleashing one of her massive revolver rounds inches from the thing's head. There was a roar of pain and I honestly thought we had hurt or killed the thing before it slashed at her, digging deep inches-deep gashes in her chest. She fell backwards, opening a clear path to the gang members who ran like hell.

It was a massacre. The thing was amongst the Ardetha gang members. Their enhanced strength drove knives into the monster's flesh, but it paid them back tenfold with its claws. One man went down as he bled out from a slashed throat. Another first lost a hand, then his head as he screamed about his stump. Olivia only got up part way and fired another point-blank shot, whipping the monster's head back. She fired again as it advanced on her, those double row of fangs dripping gore and saliva.

I leapt up in the air and landed on its back. I'd like to say it was a calculated move, but mostly I was pissed off that I couldn't seem to even annoy the thing. The animal didn't bother with me at first, but my hand became half-real claws that pulled at the invisible anchors binding its soul to its flesh. Something about the anchors was wrong, and they snapped back in place despite my efforts, driving the predator in me over the edge in rage and hunger. We kept reaching out for them, but the anchors were far stronger than any animal should have, reinforced in a way we had never encountered before. I didn't have much time to contemplate the curiosity, as it turns out trying and failing to rip out someone's soul really pisses them off.

The beast roared and tried to reach me. I uttered a very manly battle cry (not a scream of terror) and held on to it's leaf-like mane for all I was worth. It bucked a few times, but wasn't able to remove me. For a moment, I thought human ingenuity might win the day. Then I saw a malicious gleam enter the cat-lizard's eyes.

Uh Oh.

The giant 500+ pound beast flopped on its side and began to roll over. I had barely enough time to try and fail to get away as the shadow of it's bulk came down at me. The brief image of my personnel file being amended 'Died as lizard jam' flashed before my eyes.

It was the front of the bar's turn to explode. That initial explosion was quickly followed by a sudden wave of force that picked up the lizard-cat like a puppet and tossed it back towards the bathrooms. Chauncey strode in like some kind of Jedi Knight, runed tattoos glowing brightly as he activated one after another. Most humans can learn telekinetic spellcraft with some training, but Chauncey was throwing it around like a man-sized battle cannon. The creature charged him, but another tattoo flared and it hit an invisible wall of force a couple feet away from him. Each tattoo faded and dulled as it was spent, but Chauncey had more than enough to spare. Another tattoo flared and he disappeared, causing the beast to stumble and cast about for the unknown threat. A second flare and Chauncey was behind the giant lizard-cat, spraying an immense swath of fire down its backside. The survivors of the brawl, officer and gang members alike, added our firepower to the mess. The beast roared in fury and then charged for the bathroom wall, reopening the hole it had made. Chauncey gave chase, streaking my in a blur of light and fury. Half of his tattoos had gone dark, but that didn't give him pause at all. There was an explosion in the distance and Olivia and I stared at each other, partially in shock.

I slowly stood up. "Do you think we should follow him?"

Olivia was holding a hand across her gut. "I can't really move right now."

The two Ardetha gang members who weren't bleeding out on the floor took that as their cue to run for it. Olivia reached out and grabbed the first one by the ankle. There was a flash from what must have been her own spellcraft tattoo and the poor bastard stiffened and fell to the ground twitching. Taser spell, I mused, a pretty smart choice for a law enforcement officer. The second guy avoided her hands, so I helpfully threw one of the unbroken beer bottles at his head, stunning him long enough for me to stumble over there. I'm ninety percent certain that was violating some departmental procedure, but I wasn't in any condition to chase anybody at that point.

Once he was secured I checked on Olivia. "Anything I can do? You don't bleed, right?"

She grimaced. I had not been aware she could feel pain. "The cuts are deep enough, I'm in danger of losing what passes for my flesh. It takes forever to replace the stuff and I've never been in danger of losing this much. We'll need to stitch it."

I gave her a confused expression. "Stitch it? You can't, I don't know, grow it back together?"

"It's not like the movies. Takes time to heal each cut and there are too many of them. There's a staple gun in my hip pouch."

"You carry a staple gun?"

"My version of a first aid kit. Just dig it out and help me."

I studied the wounds. The creature had cut

deep gashes along her belly almost to her spine. I was surprised to see there weren't any organs I could see, just the dull brassy glint of some kind of metal endoskeleton. No wonder she hadn't minded those punches. Most of her body was a single solid mass. A mass that was in danger of having giant pieces fall to the floor. I fumbled for the staple gun. "Well you should look on the bright side."

She grimaced. "I'm about to receive first aid from our department's version of the grim reaper. What's the bright side?"

I smirked. "It missed your bra."

Olivia gave me an incredulous look, then laughed. "Ow. Well I'm relieved your first aid training covers modesty."

"Is this an impolite time to tell you that I've cuffed 2 suspects to your one?"

She gave me a mock glare. "I still have a taser charge you know, and you are looking kind of suspect-like"

Chauncey came back ten minutes later, as we started processing the scene. He was breathing heavily. "Sorry I didn't get in sooner. I had to tussle with the guys they left to guard the bikes."

I was watching an emergency medical worker attempt to replace my shoddy stapling with a somewhat more professional stitching. "I take it the lizard got away?"

Chauncey nodded. "I almost had the damn thing. It turned a corner and disappeared. If it wasn't so huge, I'd swear it dodged into a building. Any idea how it knew you would be here?"

I shook my head. "I don't think we were the target. It went after the bikers first."

"That doesn't make any sense. How would it know who they were? Why would it go after Frank Owen's business associates?"

"Maybe it has a deep-seated hatred of him. It did trash his apartment and swipe his drugs."

Chauncey snorted. "Based on what? Did he flip it off after it hit the car?"

He had me there. That was the problem with the detective side of this case. The beast was intelligent and cunning, but none of its actions matched a logical motive. Why go after Frank Owen's life? Why hunt down his friends?

Chauncey interrupted my pondering. "Any word from the suspects?"

"The veterans aren't saying anything and the newer ones don't know anything. We'll let them all sit on their laurels overnight. Someone will break."

Olivia groaned as she leaned against the

remains of the bar. "So we don't know why it does what it does, how to stop it, or where it'll strike next."

Chauncey shrugged and waved a hand dismissively. "Trust me, kid. All the answers become obvious in time. It's onl;y a matter of how many people die before you get them."

Our banter was interrupted by a hail from one of the emergency workers. To my disbelief the older biker I had dubbed 'The Squirrel' was being carried out of the rubble of the bathroom. I had assumed he had been the first kill the Beast had made, but instead he was physically unharmed.

Physically, but not mentally.

His twitching was wildly out of control now, and he rocked back and forth in front of the chair the emergency crew had placed him in. He muttered a steady litany of words I couldn't make out from our current distance.

I walked closer and the madman didn't react to my presence, but his words continued at maddening speed. "He said. He said. He said. Doom comes. He said."

I put a hand on his shoulder and he flinched before looking at me. Before he could resume rocking, I grabbed his chin and stared straight into his eyes.

The gang member's eyes were wild, almost shaking with terror. He didn't flinch when I took my glasses off, instead staring into my dark orbs as if they might hold an answer he desperately sought. Not an answer. An oblivion, maybe. Squirrel knew he was dead and was terrified dying would hurt. His pleading eyes were looking for a mercy he didn't believe was coming.

I started slowly. "What did he say?"

"He said… He said that doom would come. He said it would come and it came."

Ok. That wasn't much. I tried a different tactic. "Who said doom would come?"

Squirrel stared at me like I hadn't heard him correctly. "You know who. He said it was our fault. Our fault that she died. We didn't even know her, but that doesn't matter! He said. He said Doom would come and it has! Doom on claw and fang! Doom with a thousand teeth. He said it and it was true."

I heard an intake of breath from Chauncey behind me. He spoke cautiously. "Are you talking about Frank Owens? Did Frank Owens say doom was coming?"

The poor man's mind was incapable of rational discourse. He gabbled about his coming doom, only alternating between whether it was coming for everyone or only himself. We weren't getting any more information out of him tonight.

Chapter 18

A quick cell phone call to the Captain confirmed we should call it a night. I waited for Olivia's stitching to finish and she drove me home. We had almost finished driving to my place when I finally couldn't hold my thoughts back any more. "Are you ok? I was worried you might have been dying when you didn't get back up."

She shrugged. "I don't know if I can die, even if something took out the machinery under the flesh. I've stopped worrying about it. How about you? No normal person could take blows like that and keep moving."

"The injuries weren't as terrible as they looked. Nothing broken, but a lot of sprained and bruised muscles. My condition will have me up and running in a few hours. It'll still hurt, but I won't be limping."

Olivia checked some of the staples in her side. "Think our durability is why Captain Al-Radke requested us? Seems like a useful trait in this job."

"I doubt it. Chauncey appears to be a one-man SWAT team without us. Seriously, I know any stock human can become relatively proficient at telekinesis, but he is a whole another level there. Some of the things he did there, using spell tattoos as batteries - I didn't know it was possible."

I saw her eyebrows raise. "How did you know he...? Oh, right. Freaky eye powers"

"Big talk from the She-Hulk"

"Don't be silly. She-Hulk is a lawyer."

"Really?"

Olivia rolled her eyes towards the ceiling. "Of course I get assigned the partner that's never read a comic book before. Next you'll ask me what a movie is."

I did my best caveman impersonation. "Scary light-pictures move due to dark sorcery. Must arrest the witch with the projector first." She swatted at me.

I grew grim. "On an honest note. I don't know why he picked us for this post. I don't know what your specialty was in the academy, but mine was Organized Crime studies. I wasn't exactly expecting a post to a small town like this."

"Mine's in Mana-tech forensics. At least yours has been relevant to the case."

I sighed and spit out the taste of blood and

ceiling dust. "For a quick speech on Ardetha Gangs in general. That's what bugs me. We've been at this for 2 days and the killer is still out there. Worse, it might be following the directions of Frank Owens himself. There were 4 casualties tonight, 5 if you count the older guy's sanity. The toll is only going to go up, but I don't know where or how to stop it."

Olivia released a sigh from deep within her chest and I realized she must have been feeling the same way. "Not like the Television, is it? We've learned the creature and Frank Owens are involved with each other in some way, we know he'll likely continue hunting the Ardetha gang, but not where the gang members will be. They sure as hell won't go back to the bar."

"They'll lie low. There should be a contact or local business partner putting them up, even if they are only renting out a piece of their home and making introductions for a discrete fee. They'll hole up there until they feel the police attention has passed."

"Well, that's something to think about at least. It feels weird we are racing to save the lives of a bunch of people we also want to arrest."

"Tell me about it. Ardetha is a very dark drug, even by gang standards. In Detroit, the gangs kill Ardetha users on sight if they can. The bastards have to stick it out in middle and upper-class neighborhoods if they want to live. If I hadn't sworn the oath, I might be tempted to keep up the tradition."

"Keep it up? Have you done it before?"

I didn't answer. It was a little too close to those elements of my past I don't like to think about. Instead I motioned towards my mailbox. "We're here. Thanks for the ride Olivia - and for the backup at the bar."

She didn't answer me, instead looking out the passenger side window. "Marcus..."

I looked at the house, trying to follow her gaze. It appeared normal, the usual shades of black and white I had seen before. I followed her gaze to the side of the house and detected the smell of fresh paint. "There's something painted there. What does it say?"

Olivia swallowed. "'No Monsters'. It has some kind of symbol too."

I leaned m head back against the seat. "Wonderful. I'll deal with it in the morning."

"You don't want me to wait with you? That has got to be a hate crime."

I exhaled slowly, letting some of my frustration out between my teeth. "It is a hate crime, but there's not much we can do about it right now and nothing short of several buckets of house paint will make it go away by morning."

"Will it be safe for you to stay there?"

I shrugged and got out of the car. "If they were brave enough to face me, they wouldn't be painting the side of the house all passive-aggressive like."

With my false bravado, Olivia was reassured enough to let me go. I didn't tell her I'd be sleeping within arms-reach of my pistol. Instead I waved her off and called up the general police line, reporting the incident. It took a while before anyone could respond, but thirty minutes later a Mhanke Heights Police Department cruiser came up the street. It stopped in front and a bored-looking officer ambled out of the car. He was about medium height, with a swept back haircut and a slightly rumpled uniform. He held a half-drunk coffee in one hand and rolled his eyes lazily over at the side of the house. "You Mr. Black?"

I had removed my badge for courtesy's sake, but was still wearing my uniform. I offered my hand. "Yes. I'm glad you could come."

He didn't take the offered hand. "Weaponized People are the ERC's jurisdiction."

"Under normal circumstances I'd agree, but this would be a conflict of interest, wouldn't it?"

"I suppose so. You know who did it?"

"My neighbor, possibly. He seems to have strong opinions about me."

The officer grunted at my comment. "Mr. Griffin has been a Mhanke citizen for years. Disliking dangerous people is hardly a crime."

I waved my hand at the graffiti. "Surely, this bears investigating."

"I have to take a picture, but vandalism isn't high on our list of priorities."

I felt useless frustration rising inside of me. My other half stirred, sensing the possibility of violence. I shoved it back down, not needing the additional provocation. "This is more than mere vandalism, officer."

The man titled his head in an eye roll I could feel from two feet away. "Look. We can't call up half the town asking if people feel threatened by living next to a monster."

My voice rose at the insult. "I'm not a monster."

He ignored me. "I'll take a picture and make a report. You want anything else you can take it up with Captain Braugher."

I wanted to yell at him, but there wasn't anything I could do. Protesting to the captain would look like internal politics and strictly speaking, there wasn't any proof I could offer towards a perpetrator. I just shook my head and strode into the house. I didn't even bother to see if he took the damned picture.

Chapter 19

I slept fitfully that night, but better than I had before this case had started at least. Graffiti aside, the house was more room than I'd ever had to myself my entire life. In the morning, I managed to get up with only a minimum of self-aggrandizement, and enjoyed the beauty of a private shower with actual hot water. The academy had hosted a lot of advanced technology but had infamously underpowered water heaters. I was looking over my kit for the day when I realized that I hadn't actually managed to take time to clean my firearm. It was sloppy, I knew, but in all the excitement I hadn't even thought about such basic maintenance tasks.

The gun was a Rutger Freedom Mark II, produced in 2024. Despite the fancy name, it was really more of a standard issue nine-millimeter advertised to law enforcement for its accuracy. Like most law enforcement officers, I had more than a passing interest in firearms, but had opted for cheap reliability rather than anything fancy. The gun came apart easily under my hands as I started to clean the various pieces. We had all been issued Mark Is for our training classes and had spent almost as much time cleaning the damn things as we had shooting them. The familiar actions were carthaic, something I could perform while sitting in an unfamiliar environment working in an unfamiliar job.

I would probably have to buy a larger caliber firearm at some point. I knew some ExoReality Containment officers carried carbines, short barreled rifles with large caliber shot specifically designed to damage larger than human targets. I should ask Olivia where if her hand cannon came in a more practical size.

I had just about finished the maintenance when the doorbell rang. I jumped. Having never lived in a normal house, I had honestly forgotten that doorbells were a thing. Carefully holstering my firearm, I peeked out the door's peephole.

Two young men stood there. The first was a studious looking African-American kid with a close-shaved goateee and wild, curly hair. His companion was a wiry, pale young man holding a donut box. I briefly considered that they might be from the Anti-IWP crowd, but who brings donuts to a protest? I opened the door slightly and peered out at them. "Can I help you boys?"

The pale kid took one look at me and beamed to his partner. "You were right, James. He is a cop!"

James rubbed the bridge of his nose in irritation. "Steve. I told you he was."

Steve seemed nonplussed. "When the hot cop dropped you off, we had a bet going if you were a cop or a suspect."

'Hot Cop'. Olivia was going to hate that one, I was certain, and made a mental note to harass her about it at some point. I shrugged my shoulders. "I'm with the ExoReality Containment agency. Is there something I can help you with?"

Steve was clearly one of those people whose enthusiasm let him bowl right over anyone's reservations, glaring eyes or subtle warnings. He didn't even notice my hesitation and talked right on. "I'm Steve and this is James. We're your neighbors! Well, the other side from Mr. Griffin. We saw the paint and thought we'd offer our condolences."

He opened the box and there was a half dozen donuts in it along with a taped piece of paper bearing a message of some kind. I shook my head, not certain if I should be touched or annoyed. The donuts did look tasty, however, and I hadn't done any grocery shopping since arriving in town. Some quick mental math said I had about 30 minutes before I needed to be at the station, so I opened the door all the way and motioned them inside. James was polite enough to thank me, but Steve bowled right in like he'd been coming over for years.

Steve glanced around confused. "Why are all the lights off?"

I had wondered what the state of the lights were. I can't tell with my vision. I motioned to the light switch on the wall. "I have a visual impairment. I'm afraid I don't have much right now, but do you guys want a glass of... er... water?"

They shook their heads in the negative and sat on a pair of folding chairs I had arranged in the otherwise empty dining room. Steve eyed the pieces of my pistol cleaning kit on the counter and his eyes lit up. "Hey James, this guy has a gun! Maybe he'll be a customer!"

I reappraised the quieter kid, who was probably in his early 20s. "You sell firearms?"

He pointed at his shirt. I sighed and pointed at the sunglasses. "Vision impairment. It's all a blur to me, kid."

Steve eyes lit up like a kid on Christmas, but I pointedly looked at James to forstall him. James cleared his throat. "I work at Milton's 2nd Amendment store. It's a gun shop and a legal consul if you can believe it."

I took a moment to try and wrap my head around legal advice sold by the same person who also provided lethal weapons. "I can understand selling guns, but is there much call for legal counsel since federal open carry was passed?"

The question got James out of his shell a little bit. "Sure. I mostly sell the guns, but I'm studying law at the college. Mrs. Reilly helps advise people on things like when you can brandish, what homemade modifications are legal, and warrant related stuff."

I leaned back in the chair. It bore thinking about. Firearm ownership was up all across the globe and many governments had given up trying too hard to regulate them. What was the point of arresting someone for carrying a pistol when they could do as much damage with a telekinetic spell or a previous hidden rift-change? America technically allowed open carry of registered pistols and hunting rifles, but I guess there was still plenty of laws on the books for people to argue about. I grabbed a donut from the box and thought back to my recent frustration with stopping power/

"I might have to stop by sometime, it would be helpful to talk about options once I get a paycheck."

James smiled, but Steve had apparently stayed quiet for as long as he was capable. His voiced exploded out of him like a steam valve. "How come you can't see well? Isn't sightedness a requirement to be a cop?"

I tapped the glasses. "It's mostly a problem with color and reading. I got a waiver."

I swear the kid was vibrating with excitement at this point. "Is it because you're an IWP?"

James held a mortified expression at the blunt question. Steve misunderstood his friend's facial expression. "Not that we have any problem about that. Our friend Jasmine is an IWP. She's a…" He fumbled for the word and couldn't find it. He peered over at James for help.

James sighed and lowered his head in defeat. "She's a hexer, Steve."

Damn, I thought, that had to suck. In the nine official categories of IWP, Hexers were the rarest and probably worst off. Their abilities could fire off with any strong emotion and had a nasty habit of cursing whoever the hexer was upset at the time. The worst part was that the power could be used accidentally in an emotional moment, leading a lover's quarrel to abruptly become a case of magical assault. At least I got some advantages from my condition, but hexers could never use their powers in a normal fashion. I briefly considered the effort it would take to avoid Steve's interest and relented instead. "I'm a void-touched, do you know what that means?"

He gushed. "You got voices in your head. Can you do the cool shadow thing like Static on *Hold the Line?*"

"The real Static can't even do what the character on that show does. The only real 'shadow' thing I've got is my eyes. Let's me see mana flowing around. Not a wise trade off for becoming colorblind, though." Saying my powers only affected my vision was a baldfaced lie, but they didn't need to the darker details.

"So, you don't know what color of shirt I'm wearing?"

"No and before you ask, I'm not going to guess."

"That's cool." Steve said, clearly disappointed. "Anyway, we were sorry to see Mrs. Sharpton's house get painted like that. Some people get weirded out by the rift-changed."

"I've heard. Any idea who might have done it?"

"Not Mr. Griffen next door, if you are thinking of him. He's all pro-government in his head. He hates IWPs but he won't so much as litter. Probably some of the kids at the high school."

James explained, "We had like a dozen rift-changed in our graduating class, including Jasmine. The city council tried to pass a law segregating them from the other students but it didn't work. There's a certain group of kids every year who try to prove how brave and anti-rift they are. Don't see a difference between normal people who are different and the giant lizard that ate The Last Line."

I winced. "Is it on the news already?"

Steve's excitement boiled up again. "It's a small town. Were you there? It sounded like the thing was huge, man. My buddy Hawkins says it was bigger than a bus."

"Not as giant as that. We are going to catch it before it can cause any more damage."

"Cool, Cool. Hey, do you think you'll have it caught by Friday?"

I grimaced. "Why, is there a pool going?"

Steve smirked. "Not that I'm aware of. It's just that we— James, Me, and the other guys in our flat —play WarMages on Friday nights at a store called FLGS off main street. It's like a block from here."

I had seen the store briefly; it had a giant cardboard cutout of a massively muscled barbarian smoking a cigar and wielding a comically oversized gun on the side walk. I had assumed it was a comic book store of some kind.

"Is WarMages a video game? I can't really play those."

Steve's excitement was clearly at some kind of conversational high. "Naw, man. It's a multiplayer tabletop miniature role playing..."

James cut in again. "It's like a board game. If you want to play or hang out, we gather at 6:00pm at the store. Your partner is invited to, of course."

I hadn't a clue what kind of game this was, but my condition didn't normally give me much trouble with board games provided someone read out the text to me. It sounded far more upper class and nerdy than anything I had ever done in my life, but hell it wasn't like going down to a bar and getting shitfaced was still on the menu - especially now I had the badge. "Sure, I'll give it a shot if I can. I can't promise anything with my job, but if I'm not working, I'll drop on by."

That seemed to make them happy and they wished me 'good hunting' as we left the house. I wasn't terribly certain about their invitation, but it got them out of the house. I would be lying if I said the whole encounter hadn't warmed me back up to the neighborhood a little bit. It wasn't a fruit basket, but I could tell Olivia that at least some of my neighbors weren't looking to run my out of town in someone's trunk.

Chapter 20

I arrived only slightly late. Olivia greeted me as I came in. I noticed she had headphones around her neck and was finishing typing. I grimaced. "Did you get asked to transcribe my report?"

My answer came from Captain Al-Radke. "We don't have a transcriptionist on staff here. One of the hazards of being a medium-sized town is that we sometimes have to wear multiple hats. Don't worry about it, we'll have a better long-term solution after this case. I heard about the graffiti, did the police take a report?"

I gave a dismissive motion. "I'm certain it's already been filed under a stack of 'do not bother' somewhere."

The captain sighed. "I wish it wasn't true, but rift-changed are still controversial, even out here on the coast where the percentage of the population goes up every year. Innate Weaponized People are a favorite target for people who wish the world to go back the way it was. Any clue as to the perpetrators?"

I dropped into my chair and fumbled with the

desk holster. "'Punk Kids' seems to be the default assumption around here."

The captain tapped his pen against his desk. "Possibly. If we can help, we will. I personally try to help our rift-changed whenever I can. Even outside the job. Drives me nuts to see stuff like this happen, especially to one of our own."

"Well, at least I got to meet some neighbors who don't want me run out of town. Invited me over to play something call WarMagic or something along those lines."

Olivia's head snapped around like an owl spotting a mouse. Her eyesbrows shot up in excitement. "Did you mean WarMage?"

"Sounds about right. Like a board game?"

She held up one of the small figures which sat under her computer monitor. I leaned over and peered at the tiny miniature. It was a tiny man clad in some kind of futuristic space armor. I noticed he had little tusks to go with the oversized rifle he was holding up. I took a guess. "Is this a piece from the game?"

She nodded and waved the figure around. "I even painted him myself. It's a limited edition Captain Perspicacious of the 3rd Orcish People's brigade."

I smirked. "I understood exactly zero percent

of that sentence, but they did tell me I could bring the 'Hot Cop' which dropped me off last night."

There was booming laughter from Chauncey as he almost fell out of his chair. He clapped in glee. "Oh man. I bet it was Steve and his gang! They are a bunch of local college students who play down at FLGS."

I raised an eyebrow. "How do you know about them?"

He chuckled. "Most of them are amateur spell programmers. I actually have a set of War Mage space orcs around here somewhere form when I used to play. Still see them sometimes on Friday nights."

"Why would you have your own set? Don't they come in the box?" I asked, a little confused.

Olivia had the better question for Chauncey. "What are you doing in a gaming store on Friday nights? And why do you have a set in the office?"

Al-Radke shook his head and indicated some of the boxes in the back of the office. "One of his ex-girlfriends threw his butt out onto the street a couple years ago. He failed to take everything to his new place when he got back on his feet. As for why he's there on Friday nights." His voice took on a serious yet mocking tone. "Whatever would the Adventurers of Duntar do without their loyal Elvish Ranger?"

Chauncey shrugged. "I still play RPGs out there about twice a month when my group meets."

Nerds. I was surrounded by white collar nerds. I sighed inwardly. "Any chance RPG stands for Rocket Propelled Grenade?"

The captain saw my exasperated expression and offered a little sympathy. "You might as well get used to it. Until a year ago, the only place anyone could learn to be a real wizard was the ERC academy. A lot of our fellow officers are into fantasy stuff. If it is any consolation, I haven't played any of the junk either."

I chose to deflect the topic away from the point on hand. My childhood had involved very different fantasies, like eating three square meals and not getting evicted by the latest landlord. "Well, it's on Friday at 6 if you want to come, Olivia. I'm certain they'll be glad to see the 'Hot Cop'."

It was her turn to sigh. "I suppose it's too much to hope for one of them being a 'Hot Medical Student'? I'll be there."

Whoops. I had expected her to reject the invite. Now I would be obligated to show up myself.

Olivia ambled over to Chauncey and began to pepper him with questions about his Space Orcs until the Captain cleared his throat. "Not to interrupt our family bonding moment, but we do have an active case. More importantly, I've got a lead I want our two new agents to follow up while Chauncey and I look into a couple things." He motioned at Olivia and pulled a piece of paper out of his pocket. "It's important we find out where the Ardetha coven is hiding. It is a safe bet the beast is hunting them and I don't want a bloodbath if the two forces duke it out in the middle of town. I got a call this morning from the hospital. We've had an observation request in with their admin, asking them to let me know if anyone shows up with Ardetha-like symptoms. We are in luck, as the parents of one Abigail Smithson forcibly checked her in. She has developed a major light sensitivity and 2 inch long fangs, sound familiar?"

Olivia reached for the paper eagerly. "Someone who's started the treatments. A recruit."

I ran over to my desk and pulled a few supplies. "The gang will only give the treatments in a secure location to avoid discovery. Probably the same location they are hiding in now."

Mike nodded. "My thoughts exactly. Get over there and see if you can convince her to tell you where she got the treatments." He paused before ushering us out the door. "It is a decent theory you two have and I'm glad you did the research and adjusted accordingly. This is exactly the kind of flexible thinking I wanted when I requested you two. Excellent work, but keep flexible. Not every theory pans out."

With both the praise and warning in our minds, we headed downstairs to the car.

Chapter 21

My mind whirled on the possibilities as Olivia drove us to the hospital. The Ardetha patient could blow the case wide open if they knew where the gang was holed up. I thought over what I knew; Recruitment and transformation into a member of the gang wasn't instantaneous - you needed multiple treatments to get all the changes. Total transformation would generally take five to seven treatments in total, with the final treatment triggering the most extreme changes. The first three injections would have only slight effects - a faster metabolism, massive fat loss followed by muscle gain, and a slower, paler parlor to the skin. Just enough changes to get the recruit excited for more. The fangs would come in around the fourth treatment. It was for the fourth treatment when the recruit would normally leave their friends and family and move in with their alternate family. The user couldn't hide their physiological changes by that point and the treatments weren't reversible. This kid must have come home or been caught outside the gang's hideout.

I was unsurprised to find out the kid had been assigned to an underpopulated ward of the hospital and there was a security guard at the ward entrance. Even without all the treatments, an Ardetha user would already have enough strength and enhanced aggressiveness to cause a lot of harm if they got loose. We walked up to the lone nurse, whose nametag read 'Bambi'. She looked nothing like you'd expect from the name, all hard muscles and a stern expression which would have displayed more at home on a bouncer than a medical professional. I noticed the security guard only addressed her in the politest terms and I resolved to do the same.

The woman eyed us warily. "You aren't Chauncey."

I pulled out my Agency ID out from my pocket. "I'm Detective Black and this is Detective Baer. We are recent additions to the department." I elected to omit the 'Junior' next to the 'Detective', there was no need to drag out the semantics after all.

"Huh. Little rat Chauncey still doesn't want to see me and risk another kick to his knockers, does he? Your patient is in room 12 at the end of the hall. She's restrained so she doesn't try to kill everyone."

I dearly wanted to find out what common history Bambi and Chauncey had shared that ended with 'a kick to his knockers', but we didn't have enough time. A mischievous grin on Olivia's face told me she'd remember to ask Chauncey when the opportunity presented itself. "Anything we should know before we go in? Is she sedated?"

Bambi snorted. "Can't risk sedation until her DNA results get back - might have an undocumented allergy or something. She hasn't tried anything so far, probably still weak after the 'treatment'. Just call if she tries to murder you." She emphasized the last word with a couching of her fingers.

We thanked the nurse and headed down the hall. Olivia paused and waved a hand at me. "You're the gang expert, how do you want to do this?"

"Ardetha users are way more than members of a gang, but I'll take the lead. Hopefully she'll be cooperative."

In the doorway sat Abigail Smithson on her hospital bed. She had been one of those plain girls that young boys liked to tease in high school. Her figure was tall, with thin limbs and a square torso which made her appear older than she was. The Ardetha treatments had clearly been to work on her body and her thinness was now accentuated by wiry muscles and dark circles under her eyes. I noticed her hair was shifting from a ginger red to black, and the lights in the room had been turned down to a dim glow. She looked helpless and alone lying there in the hospital bed but looks could be deceiving.

Her eyes, pupils dilated to abnormal size, shifted between us. She peered at Olivia hopefully. "Did you bring the milkshake? I'm due for another."

It took me a moment to realize she must be on a liquid diet. Starting about last year, many of the most recent Ardetha users who had been picked up could no longer handle raw food. Their metabolism had been needlessly adapted to the consumption of blood and liquid nutrient supplements. Dr. Partridge was getting close to achieving his vampire legend. I shook my head at the inquiry and bulled on ahead. "How many treatments have you had?"

She looked like a teenager that had been caught in the naughty movie section of a store, not someone who had taken a dangerous DNA serum. "I don't know what's happened. I just got..."

I snorted derisively. "Can it. You've been getting Ardetha injections."

Olivia shuffled next to me, uncomfortable at my aggression. The kid's head turned away, unable to meet my eyes. I pushed forward. "Look - any blood test is going to show the markers, so let's cut the bullshit. Are you on your fourth treatment or your fifth?"

She continued to stare at her hands. "Fourth. Getting the treatments isn't a crime, you know."

I was familiar with the responses dealers fed to

their customers. Most of it was junk designed to ease their worries over getting caught and to encourage them not to tell the police anything useful. "Getting treatments isn't a crime, but possessing the drug and dealing it is. So why don't you tell me who your dealer was?"

The kid panicked. "I can't tell you that."

"C'mon kid. You don't want to get in trouble. Tell us who your dealer is? Who did you buy the treatments from?"

She whined. "I can't!"

I could feel anger building up inside me. All the frustration over the case, the deaths, even the prejudice sprayed over the house began to rise in me. This kid had signed on to become a monster, but she was the only way I could find the Ardetha gang. Olivia put a hand on my shoulder but I shrugged it off. Instead I lowered myself over the bed, gritting my teeth. "Why. Not?"

She cried. "I still need two more treatments!"

The confession broke her down and she began sobbing. I couldn't believe what I was hearing. I yelled, "You still want the treatments? You want to become one of them?"

I was about to continue my tirade when there was a calm, insistent hand on my arm that wouldn't let go. I tried to shake Olivia off again, but her arm didn't budge. I glared daggers at my partner, but she returned my glare with her own cool, steady eyes. "I think we need to step out now."

"We need..." I protested.

The tug became insistent and I had to follow her to avoid being lifted off the floor. The girl was weeping at this point anyway.

I followed Olivia for a couple rooms and then we ducked into an empty patient room. She waved her hands in the air. "What the hell was that?"

"What?"

"I thought you didn't like being called a monster."

I winced, the name had slipped out in the conversation. "Hey, I didn't choose to become what I am. That kid in there has volunteered to be a genetically modified cannibal."

"The kid is not a cannibal." Olivia pointed in the direction of the room.

"You clearly don't know how this works. If she gets those treatments, she'll be constantly desiring blood. Most of them have no compunction about snacking on a person or two if they get the chance."

"We need her help."

That was the part which pissed me off the most, "You think I don't know that? She's a vampire recruit. She won't betray her gang as long as she thinks they can get her a treatment. What are you going to do, appeal to her better nature?"

For the first time, Olivia glared at me disapprovingly, "I don't know what your history or problem with her kind is, but you need to let it go. She's a child and if we had been a little more understanding about where she was coming from, she might just have helped us out"

"I don't think she would, Olivia. You don't know these people."

"I know you, don't I?"

The comment set me off. I got right up in Olivia's face. "I have done terrible things in my past Olivia. Terrible things. I would never have signed up to be what I am. That's the difference. I drove a car down the wrong street at the wrong time - she freaking volunteered for it. She wants to be the tragic monster and is willing to let people get hurt along the way."

Olivia shook her head and let the matter drop. "Look. This isn't getting us anywhere. Let's head back to the office."

I paused. "Actually I do have something." I pulled a pink cell phone out of my pocket.

"Did you steal her cell phone?"

"No. That would be an unauthorized search and seizure. I just found this phone and am going to scroll through the call log to see who she's been talking to."

I pulled out my phone and activated my reader app. I was about two menus into the complicated process of getting one phone to read another's screen and give me verbal prompts, when Olivia rolled her eyes and swiped the girl's phone from me. "You should have called in for a warrant," she stated, and started navigating down the list of recent contacts. "Family, family, someone called Sarah, someone called Bobby, what the heck are you looking for?"

"Search for a raw phone number without a contact ID attached to it. There will be a lot of recent calls to it. It won't have a contact because she wants deniability about who is calling her."

"There's only one like that. 555-4832."

I made a mental note of the number. "Excellent, let's turn this missing phone into the Lost and Found downstairs and query that number in the case system."

"Why not give it to the nurse?"

"Because I don't want her warning anyone right away. Also, that was a terrible excuse I gave you and I know it."

Chapter 22

We headed out. Olivia didn't say anything, but we both knew I had screwed up the interrogation. Seeing the Ardetha user had brought back a lot of awful memories, not just the recent ones. I hadn't been kidding when I told her Ardetha users were feared and hunted in the Detroit slums. Just looking at the fangs had reminded me of the half-whispered stories of disappearing people, of dealers who turned up as dry husks, and revenge hits by local gangs. Back then I couldn't understand why someone would undergo such a terrible change, and I understood it even less now. It was one thing to read about the tragic vampire of fiction, lonely but beautiful people who needed to kill to survive. It was a whole another level of narcissism to decide to become one. To put your own desire for power and beauty above the well-being of innocent people. No matter what Olivia thought, the girl in the hospital bed was one of the worst kinds of monster and I had been unable to put that behind me for the interrogation.

I called it in as Olivia drove the car. Chauncey picked up and started the submission to get a search warrant with the cell phone company. We had almost reached the station when his voice abruptly perked up. "Hey. I got a hit in our local database. Apparently, our dealer doesn't know the point of burner phone is to throw it away after you get picked up. John Waters. He was picked up by Judy, one of the beat officers down on the south part of town. I'll get her to meet you out there."

That was the best news we'd gotten all day. I thanked Chauncey and passed the information along to Olivia. It was across town, but Mhanke heights had a population slightly less than a hundred thousand so it wouldn't take very long to meet the police officer. I spent the time examining this unfamiliar town I found myself in. We went down main street, with its older buildings and modestly-sized shops to the newer southern portion of the town. Here stood three and four story apartment buildings, quickly constructed over the past few years as people converged in the protected urban areas. They were dour counterpoints to the previous buildings, built for expediency rather than beauty. Even in a smaller-sized town like Mhanke Heights there is room for poverty and desperation. People who lost their livelihoods in rift events gathered here and not all of them had found the same economic level of work as they had before. More than one former farmer counted themselves lucky if they got a job as a stock clerk or shipping worker. Graffiti would be endemic here and part of me wished I could see it, both for the familiarity of it and to see if any of the styling matched the side of my house.

Olivia pulled us into the parking lot of a corner store. A pair of beat officers stood there, leaning against a scratched police cruiser. I waved a hello as we parked. I didn't get a wave back, but they seemed friendly to our presence. The woman officer, who was the older of the two, peered over at us and remarked, "I heard Mike had new blood. Don't take it wrong, but I was kinda hoping you'd have brought Chauncey with you."

I cocked my head. "Why?"

"Because he's cuter than you, kid."

Olivia broke out laughing. She swatted me across the back of my chest with the back of her hand. "It seems like every woman in this town knows who Chauncey is. Popular man."

Judy snorted. "Have you seen the other male officers? Even a mediocre steak looks tasty amongst a bunch of hamburger."

Okay, this conversation needed to be deterred before it went somewhere I did not want to be standing around for. For both myself and the other male officer I cleared my throat. "Um, I believe we are looking for a Mr. John Waters?"

Judy threw up her hands in frustration. "I remember the snot. Has tattoos and dressed like he'd seen a James Dean movie once in his life and plotted his wardrobe accordingly. Kid has fangs, but that's not too unusual these days. Picked him up for tagging a car to impress some girls."

"No arrest?"

Judy shrugged. "I took down him to the station, but minor crimes like that get an automatic bail set if noone can tie it to a larger crime. Someone posted it within hours, probably an older sibling."

More likely an older member of the gang, I thought. Posting bail and then having the bailee work off the 'debt' was a normal part of gang life. "Any idea where he hangs out?"

"A couple blocks down at a local poolhall called 'Double Eights'. A lot of neighborhood kids hang out there before curfew."

We thanked Judy for the information and started walking towards the car when a massive cracking boom echoed down the street. The four of us stared at each other for a moment, realizing the sound had come for the direction Judy had just indicated. Our group ran around the corner and saw, to our disbelief, John Waters running down the street as fast as he could.

His genetically enhanced legs propelled him at an impressive sprint, but it was only keeping him mere meters away for the giant snapping fangs behind him. It seemed the Beast had found the teen mere moments before we had.

The two beat officers didn't hesitate, but

attempted to put themselves between the Beast and John while unloading with their sidearms. Olivia and I attempted to draw it off by firing at its head. The unexpected firepower from Olivia's revolver cowed the giant leafy lizard for a moment, but then it riled back up and started charging forward again. In desperation, I grabbed one of the leaf-like projections from the side of the animal as it raced past. There was a painful wrenching sensation from my shoulder as I became airborne. I only had a brief glimpse of my companions running back for their cars as apartment buildings flashed past on either side. Cars screeched to a halt and crashed into each other as the Beast trampled traffic underfoot. I scrabbled at the side of the beast and managed to use the leaf-flaps as hand holds to mount myself onto the creature's back.

That pissed it off. The Beast slammed itself against a nearby light pole in an attempt to shake me off. I pulled into the spaces within myself and let my other half have more control. My left hand turned dark as shadows enveloped it and claws formed to hook into the beast's flesh. The monster roared in pain, but I still held on. John Waters was starting to slow down, but the Beast's distraction meant it had was not catching up. I let go with my left hand, trusting my right to hold me on as I drew my firearm. Nine-millimeter bullets hadn't done much so far, but a shot to the back of the head should slow down anybody. The Beast bucked again and I almost went flying, feeling another jolt of pain as I struggled to stay on.

John Waters finally tripped, spilling out onto the concrete median. I desperately lined up the shot as the Beast realized its prey was finally run to ground. Almost there, I almost had the shot.

Then the world exploded in pain as something hot and fierce cut into my left arm. I think I cried out as I fell off the beast and slid to the ground. I barely had time to register what had happened when a crack and pinging sound echoed mere inches from me ear. Someone was shooting at me. Somewhere in the street was a scream. I rolled myself to the side and scrambled for a parked car as cover while two more pinging sounds echoed off the pavement. I dragged myself behind the car and winced as another bullet went straight through the car and splashed somewhere to my left. Whoever this was, those shots came from something more than a mere hunting rifle. I desperately searched the nearby buildings but couldn't locate the shooter, drawing only another near miss for my troubles. I wanted to shoot back, but shooting blind could get a lot of innocent people hurt. The shot from the car had passed nearly parallel to my position, so the shooter had to be somewhere in the apartment building across the street.

There was the sound of sirens as Judy, Olivia, and the male officer whose name I couldn't remember came screeching up the street, Judy impressivly driving on the sidewalk for at least some of the distance. The officers came out with guns drawn and the shooting stopped. I risked sticking my body up long enough to wave to Olivia before slumping down next to the car.

She came sprinting around the corner and gave a worried sound. "Jesus, Marcus. You've been hit!" She scrambled for her phone and hit the emergency dial, looking over the wound while her call connected. "Is this a bullet wound?"

I nodded my head groggily, trying to push back the pain. "Sniper. Beast had some help."

She shook her head in amazement. "Who the hell would help that thing?"

"I don't know. Did the kid get away?"

Olivia didn't answer me at first, instead pulling off my uniform shirt and getting a bandage out of a belt pouch. I tried to focus on her face. "Olivia, did the kid get away?"

She bit her lip and pulled my underlying t-shirt away from the wound. She hesitated and then shook her head as she packed gauze into the hole. "I'm sorry Marcus. He's... he's out there on the street. Most of him."

"Damn it to hell!" I cursed and slammed my fist against the car. "We needed that lead!"

Olivia appeared a little taken aback. "He wasn't just a lead Marcus, he was a human being."

"I know that Olivia. I tried to save him. I just..." I stopped and then started again. "Look, I know I screwed up getting the lead from the Ardetha girl. If I'd kept Waters alive and gotten a lead there it could have made up for it."

Olivia nodded and started talking into the phone as she connected to the emergency dispatch center. I let my head loll a little to the left and examined the wound. It was hard to tell under the bandages, but there was a lot of blood soaking the arm, even with the uniform shirt removed. A thin trail of it dribbled out from where I had crawled to the car. Damn, I thought, I really could have bought it. My eyes traveled down my arm again and settled on my hand. The shadowy void-stuff forming claws was still there. The claws were alarming. Normally the my other half could only manifest something like that for a few seconds, maybe half a minute if I was lucky. I hadn't expected to see the claw this long after action. I twitched my fingers and the claws shifted, clearly still there. I mentally reached for the other presence in my arm and tried to shove its control away from the arm.

No.

I had heard a seemingly audible voice in my head and swiveled right and left as best I was able. I tried to retract the power again, but again came an audible *No.* What the hell was this? The spirit inside of me couldn't form words, much less talk. I gathered as much willpower as I could and shove against the presence as hard as I could. There was an immediate pushback of almost as much strength as there had been after a feeding. I tried to keep my face impassive as I engaged the presence in a battle of the wills, gradually shoving it back down into its designated place within myself.

What the hell had that been about?

Chapter 23

The sound of ambulance and police sirens started blaring in my ears as Mhanke Heights responded to this latest tragedy on its streets. Judy's partner, whose name I know remembered was Kevin, had been slashed while standing in the Beasts path and we got to trade jibes as the medics loaded us in to the ambulance. He looked over at me and scoffed. "Bullet wound? Didn't you tell the bad guys you dainties are only authorized to handle magic stuff?'

I couldn't help it. I chuckled a little and said, "Didn't they tell you beat cops to stop getting involved in ERC cases?"

He didn't skip a beat. "Hey. That lizard was clearly going the wrong direction against traffic. *You* interfered in my perfectly legitimate attempt to ticket his ass. Total copblock."

"Copblock?"

Kevin titled his nose in the air. "Perfectly valid word. I made it up myself."

I decided I liked Kevin, which is an odd

feeling since he likely would have arrested me if we had met a few years ago. I mumbled off something about veteran officers interfering with rookies for sport and drifted off as the painkillers flooded up my uninjured arm. I dreamt briefly, remembering an eternal void which wasn't really a void and of eternal hunters chasing each other throughout a starless universe. The dream was starting to feel uncomfortably like home.

My stay in the hospital was brief. They sewed up the bleeding hole in my arm and rebandaged it. I had to wait a couple hours while they waited for the painkillers to flush out of my system, but it gave me time to think. I took the opportunity to call Victor.

There was a click after the second ring and a gruff voice answered, "This is Ward. Whom is calling?"

I chuckled. "You still don't have caller ID, old man?"

I only got a responding grunt and started to smile despite myself. Victor Ward had been my mentor for years since I had become rift-changed and it was an old joke between us. "Old Man? Must be Marcus, only a punk kid would insult his betters."

I snorted. "Are my betters there? Can I speak to them instead?"

The comment earned me a small laugh. "I

should make you call me captain now that you are part of the ERC. You are still employed, right? Mike wasn't forced to ship you back to the academy?"

My eyebrows raised in alarm. "Wait, can he do that?"

"Never underestimate what Al-Radke can do when he puts his mind to it."

I shifted the phone to my other hand and leaned back on the wall. "He tells me you guys knew each other."

"Know. We still talk a couple times a month. He was one of the ERC's first recruits and an ally of the FBI task force before then. Had a habit of falling into rift event cases even before they were public knowledge. Did he tell you he approached me for recommendations on filling those positions you and Olivia are in?"

"No, but I wondered. Did you recommend me?"

"Both of you. Al-Radke likes people who think on their feet and you both excel at that."

"Wait," I said. "You know Olivia?"

"No, but she was well known amongst the instructors. Very capable at detail and willing to deal with adversity."

"Well there's plenty of adversity out here. I'm on my first case and I've already been shot."

"I'm sorry to say it probably won't be a once in a lifetime incident. I've lost track of how many bullets my symbiote and I have been hit with."

I paused a moment, letting the silence drag on as I gathered my courage. There was a tightness in my chest as I spoke. "Speaking of symbiotes. That is kind of what I wanted to talk about."

Victors voice turned a little graver than before. "Has there been a change?"

"I'm not certain. You always said you could speak with yours, is that accurate?"

He mused. "Sure. It hears everything I do in addition to knowing my thoughts. I think at it and it gets the message. I thought yours couldn't form words?"

I swallowed hard. "I think it might have recently… talked to me."

"Damn. Are you certain?"

I kicked the wall behind me. "No I'm not. Is there a way to tell?"

There was a pause for a moment as Victor searched for the right words. "Not as such. You're sharing a head so it can be hard to tell what comes from your own thoughts and what comes from the void spirit. Did it feed?"

'Feed' was a kind way of asking if I had killed someone by ripping their soul from their body. I paused, not wanting to get the words out. Shame washed over me.

Victor got the message even thought if I hadn't said anything. "Self-defense?"

"Yeah, but..."

He interrupted me. "No buts. That's the rule, if someone is trying to kill you then it happens. Only so long as its self-defense. You do remember what I told you about feeding that thing, though?"

My voice came out a lot smaller than I wanted it to. It was dangerously close to a whine. "You said it might grow. What does that mean?"

"The Void-Predators are from a world with a completely different set of rules than our own. They don't age or grow by passing time like we do. They do it by feeding, growing bigger, faster, stronger, smarter with each meal. I called yours a baby, but it could be a hundred years old for all I know. When I first got stuck with mine it couldn't mutter much more than a yes or no. At best we could melt into the shadows, maybe cast some void-stuff out there if we needed to. You've seen what we can do now. Those changes came from feeding it in a career's worth of violent containment actions."

My breath caught in my chest but I forced it down. "I know you warned me about it, I'm just worried about what it means for my ability to control it."

"I'm not going to lie to you Marcus. The more you kill with it, the stronger it becomes, the more able to control you it will be. At some point, it'll stop fighting you but until then it'll do everything it can to dominate you. If it succeeds, you won't be able to reassert control. No one has."

My fists clenched. "Is there a way to weaken it? To take it back down to where it was?"

Victor's voice was serious and cold. "I'm afraid not. It gets what it needs to survive by sipping on your soul anchors. Anything extra you give it will go straight to becoming stronger."

"Damn."

My mentor's voice softened a little. "Look. I warned you about this when you chose the agency, but you hadn't experienced it yet. It's not too late to choose another profession. Some Void-Touched never use their powers. You know Cameron is still a painter?"

For a brief moment I considered it. It was a huge risk for me to be in this profession. There would inevitably be life and death situations and the thing inside me would get plenty of opportunities to grow. "I can't. I have to make things better."

"Trying to erase your past through positive deeds isn't possible Marcus."

I rubbed the phone absentmindedly. "I know, but this is about being better than my past, not erasing it."

I heard the man take a deep breath. "All right. Just promise me you'll let Mike know if it gets to be too much. I'd rather you spent your life behind a desk than running from the ERC."

That was putting it lightly. I remembered the stories Victor had told me of hunting down the two-thirds of Void-touched who had gone insane. I wavered for a moment and then steeled myself. "I know. Thank you, Victor."

"Call whenever you need. I'm almost retired now all of you academy graduates are in the field. Thinking of taking up gardening."

The brief image of the man I knew; tall, lean and wrapped in a dark ankle length coat, tending to carrots and peas brightened my day. "I bet," I said.

We said our goodbyes and I promised once again to let Mike Al-Radke know if I needed to remove myself from the job. As the line clicked off, I slid to the floor in emotional exhaustion.

I thought about my situation. The incident with my hand after the shooting might have been nothing, just some complications due to the amount of pain I was in. I couldn't shake the feeling it was more than that, that the thing inside of me was getting stronger. If it was, nothing would change. I'd fight for my right to my own mind and destiny. No matter what it cost me in the end.

Olivia came in a little while later, while I was doing my best to get my uniform shirt on. I didn't hear her coming in until there was a soft knock on the hospital room door. I turned around, partially caught in my shirt.

She laughed. "Stuck?"

I waved my wounded arm. "I'm a little disadvantaged."

She helped me into the shirt. "I'm surprised they are letting you out. That was quite a shot."

"It was actually a ricochet. The bullet was still in my arm."

"Did CSI get a hold of it?"

"Yeah, they say it was a long barreled rifle round, steel jacketed of all things."

Olivia did her signature cocked head thing again. "Are you certain they were aiming at you? Not the Beast?"

"Yeah. The shots followed me as I heroically ran for cover."

"That's not the kind of ammunition you use for killing an unarmored human."

"I was wearing a vest," I started but then thought on it some more, "but a normal round of this size would have probably done the job. Steel jacket is a weird choice since it would be less likely to kill me than a softer round."

Olivia pulled out her phone, likely connecting to our case files. I thought on the problem for a moment. Steel Jacket rounds weren't common. For all the freedom with owning and carrying firearms, it wasn't normal for anyone to carry armor piercing rounds. Only a madman would use them within city limits, where a missed round could easily punch though another wall and hit an unintended person.

It hit me and I gave a dark chuckle. "*Hold The Line*. That's why they used armor piercing ammunition."

Olivia paused, looking confused. "Isn't *Hold the Line* a TV Show?"

I nodded. "It is, about the FBI task force before the Agency. The point is that in the show, the Void-Touched character is immune to normal bullets. The only time he ever gets wounded is when someone uses armor piercing ammunition."

"I wasn't aware the void touched were bulletproof."

I smirked. "We aren't. The experienced ones can phase a little, causing bullets to pass through them. It was too complicated a concept for the show so they just had the bullets bounce off. A while later, they invented the armor piercing thing."

Olivia titled her head up incredulously. "So, our shooter got their information from a TV Show?"

"Most people do. That's why everyone thinks golems don't have emotions and why people with the elmentalist archetype are always expected to work with fire. Our shooter didn't bother to actually research his target, they went off their knowledge of pop culture."

Olivia thought about for a moment. "Their accuracy was poor too. So not an expert shooter?"

"Probably someone unused to shooting outside the range. That means they likely didn't own the rifle for long."

Olivia got excited. "Let's head to the office. I bet I can tell you who owns the rifle."

A surge of elation hit me after her comment. I eagerly signed myself out of the hospital and followed Olivia to the car.

Chapter 24

We arrived at the station a little while later and I followed my partner down to the building's basement. The basement had been given over to the Crime Scene Investigations team. The Police department may have been minuscule by Detroit standards, with only around 60 or so police officers, but it was just numerous enough to actually have a Crime Scene Investigation team. Olivia must have been making friends when I wasn't looking, because the whole team greeted her upon entry into their domain.

Don't mistake me, stepping into CSI is like stepping into another world compared to anywhere else in the station. Everything has the appearance of high school science lab, with grey granite countertops and sophisticated equipment sitting in corners. Moreover, the whole place radiates a sense of being clean. Not only a 'We clean up well around here' sense, but more like a sterile hospital office. Even the traces of mana had been filtered with a little machine humming along quietly in the corner. It's impressive and more than a little intimidating. Four people stood at the countertops, using equipment or typing away on computers.

Olivia leaned over to me conspiratorially. "We can enter as long as we wear gloves, but don't touch anything that looks like evidence without permission. They are sensitive about that here."

"Personal experience?"

She winced but didn't say anything as she donned a pair of evidence handling gloves. At least they didn't make us wear lab coats. An older woman sitting at a countertop overtly checked each of our hands as we entered, no doubt verifying we had followed the rules and donned gloves. She looked like a doll, with a lab coat and glasses slightly too big on her and an unruly shock of curly hair which was kept under a hair net. Satisfied that we were appropriately attired, she waved us in and threw a pen at a thin man stooped over a microscope. "Hey Mac! Officer Sunglasses here wants to see the bullet that nicked him!"

'Mac's head snapped up from his microscope. He was a stork of man, all hard lines that was determined to poke out at strange angles no matter what he was doing at the time. His hair was as unruly and had been hastily crammed under a baseball cap that read - I kid you not - 'Sexy Men Solve Cases'. He wore his labcoat like a second skin over a faded dress shirt and jeans. I idly wondered if I had wandered into a high school chemistry lab where someone had repurposed all the teachers. Mac carefully set down what he was looking at and packed it in a plastic box. I saw it was a bullet, but a smaller nine-millimeter shot not a sniper round like we were hoping for.

I stared at the round. "Is that one of mine?"

He shook his head. "No. Sadly you are not the only officer involved shooting today. Some moron tried to shoot his ex-wife this morning at a convenience store. I have bullets from him, the store owner, the ex-wife, and two bystanders. This open carry crap may have reduced the rate of violent crime a little, but when something does go off it becomes a CSI nightmare. I still haven't figured out which bullet is the one that knocked him off his feet."

I did some mental math. "Five shooters? Is it normal for so many people to be involved?"

He shrugged. "Most people aren't dumb enough to shoot someone in public for precisely this reason. When it does, we have a hell of a time figuring out all the guns involved. Smart killers shoot people in private, but smart killers are rare indeed."

He started pulling up images on the screen with the aid of well-worn keypad. He clicked around for a while and waved a hand at the screen. I didn't feel like telling him I couldn't see whatever he was waving at.

He spoke quickly. "You'll notice the round didn't malform much despite the high velocity. Part of that is from hitting softer hide of the animal and ricocheting into the meat of your arm."

He clicked around some more and Olivia winced. She leaned over and told me we were looking at the two inch wide hole that had been bored into my shoulder from the round. I didn't realize the shot had made that considerable of a hole. If my arm had been normal flesh at the time, I could still be in the hospital, ricochet or not. Mac noticed my discomfort and flipped back to the first image. "It's a steel jacketed round, .338 caliber. Likely fired from a long bore rifle. Daniel over there," he indicated the only member of the team not wearing a lab coat, "managed to trace the shots from a fourth-floor apartment which had been broken into. The shooter was in a terrible hurry, but we weren't able to get a positive fingerprint match. We have some DNA that doesn't match the apartment owners, but no matches in our database."

Olivia grinned, clearly happy to be discussing a topic she enjoyed. "Any chance on identifying the brand of bullet?"

Mac smiled ruefully. "We thought of that, but it was a custom build. I'm guessing someone who makes their own rounds."

"How about the powder?"

The lab-coated investigator chuckled. "Great minds think alike. I have ID'd the powder as a commercial blend from a Bakersfield, California company. Unfortunately, I would need a tightly specific time frame to get an idea of who bought the stuff. We track gunpowder coming into the city via the convoys but after that it's up to the retailers."

I interrupted, "I think this was a rushed attempt. The shooter likely built the rounds after finding out what I was."

"That would make a rather short timeline. Do you think you were the target?"

There was a grunt from Daniel. "I told you, Mac. Amateur."

I shrugged. "Likely someone upset at my IWP status."

Mac mused. "It could be. We had 5 IWPs in the city, 6 now with yourself added. The others have been harassed on occasion, but nobody has tried to shoot them before."

"We've never had an IWP with the power to arrest people before. Authority makes me much more threatening than your average IWP," I pointed out.

He nodded. "Well assuming they bought the powder sometime after you showed up, it would have come from one of the last two shipments. That leaves you with two stores, both of which are known as law enforcement friendly. If you are lucky, your suspect paid with a credit card and will be on our list of previous offenders for Innate Weaponized Personnel harassment. Most of the harassment doesn't end in an arrest, but a report is made all the same."

"Trust me, I have personal experience in just how causally local PD takes harassment."

He winced. "Sorry about that. You don't always get to see the best side of this town on the job."

I leaned against the counter. "Print me out that list of suspects. If I'm lucky, we'll help improve this town's outlook with some plain old-fashioned law enforcement."

Chapter 25

We tried to check in with Captain Al-Radke, but he and Chauncey were off following a lead somewhere. Since nobody had said we couldn't keep working, I decided to take advantage of the temporary lack of oversight to investigate my own attempted murder. Olivia and I made calls and cross-checked lists, tracking the dozen or so people who had bought their own gunpowder in the past week. I was surprised so many people made their own bullets, but I guess everyone needs a hobby. Strictly speaking, an assassination with a normal mundane rifle put the jurisdiction with the standard police department. Luckily, I knew someone in the department that had a favorable opinion of us at the moment and eagerly called up Detective Williams. The man and his partner agreed to meet us in an hour and I gratefully lowered the phone and looked over at Olivia.

"I think we have the guy. One hour, the detectives will take the lead and make the arrest, but we can interview the suspect once he's in custody."

She smiled. "That's great news. Would have

liked to been at the arrest, but I'll settle for catching a bad guy."

I grinned. "Hey! It isn't the beast, but I think this counts as our first solved case. All with heavy action phone dialing."

Olivia smirked. "If anyone asks, I'll say we wrestled a Mutagen for the information."

I laughed and leaned back in my chair. "You know, I owe you an apology my behavior at the hospital."

She raised her shoulders in an exaggerated shrugging motion. "I don't want an apology. I just wish I knew what set you off."

I sighed. "I've been thinking about that. If we are going to be partners you might as well know the whole damn package. Did you know I used to have tattoos?"

She shrugged at pointed at my uniform shirt. "I didn't know you didn't have tattoos now. What's a tattoo got to do with the Ardetha gangs?"

"I'm getting there. The point is, I got my first tattoo when I was 13. It was a gang tag and marked me as a member of a crew associated with the 486 Bloods."

She squinted at me. "I don't know what a gang tag is."

Her confession shocked me for a moment before I realized Olivia wasn't actually as old as she appeared. If what she had told me was true, she probably hadn't met a gang member before she came to Mhanke Heights. So much for beating around the bush. "I'm saying I belonged to a gang. I wasn't a minor member either. I've probably committed more felonies than most people we'll arrest."

"That..." she started. "That doesn't make sense. Do they allow people with convictions in the agency?"

"There's some precedent, but I don't actually have any convictions on my record. I suspect most of my crimes have vague witness descriptions like 'some tall, possibly Hispanic guy'. I didn't exactly stick out in a lineup and most people didn't see much past the tattoos and gang attire."

"So how does your past tie in with Abigail the Ardetha user?"

I leaned back. Olivia and I had very different pasts. I briefly wondered if it was possible to make her understand where I was coming from, but there was no helping it but to try. "Gang life hasn't changed much since the rifts started popping up for the most part. At best, we cut a few drugs with cheap mana catalyst, but still ran the same businesses and crimes. Ardetha was different. Most of us came from poor neighborhoods with no one to look out for us but our fellow gang members. Violence might break out and there might be some scuffles, but most gangs are just small, illicit businesses running in different areas. Ardetha users don't come from the poor neighborhoods usually. They like to recruit teenagers and young college kids from the middle and upper classes. People who can get normal nine to five jobs and have families who can support them if they end up laid up. I don't care how screwed up the life Abigail is running away from, it's most likely far better than the rathole I grew up in. That's the first part of what sets them apart. The first strike against them."

Olivia interrupted, "So the gangs are jealous of Ardetha Users?"

"Not really. Well maybe. It's more like we can't understand them. They had a life we would have killed for, but left it behind to wallow in our crap. Gangs are tight-knit, but I don't think many people would stay in if they had a chance for a real family with a real home and all the advantages that come with it. Where they come from sets the Ardetha gangs apart, makes them something impossible to understand."

"I guess I can see why that would cause some friction. Do the gangs fear them?"

"That would be strike two against them. Ardetha doesn't just make you stronger, it makes you meaner. Ardetha users will fight anyone, anytime, over anything. I once saw one attack a police car because the flashing lights interrupted his nap. The gangs don't like to deal with them because any interaction with them can swiftly become a massive melee. It is easier to leave them to their neighborhoods and avoid them when possible."

Olivia nodded and held up three fingers. "What's strike three?"

"They kill. You piss one off; he might kill you and everyone with you just to make a point. You have something they want; they might kill you to get it. The worst is sometimes they just murder people. Most of them prefer human blood. Even the older ones who can still eat normal food prefer to drink their lunch. When people disappeared in the Detroit hoods we'd say a Vamp got them. Most of the time we'd be right. You'd find someone's brother or sister a few days later hanging from a fence - all the blood gone. I hated it."

Olivia stirred nervously. "You said the gangs would go after Ardetha users who violated their territory?"

I leaned back, remembering the hushed meetings between crews before a hunt would be called. "We would. The belief was that you needed a ratio of five to one to get it done. Five of your guys for every Ardetha user you expected to find. Never take on more than three of those vamps at once. It was rare though. For the most part it doesn't help much. Which brings me to Abigail. She looks like a nice girl, but she's eagerly running down a path which would have her ripping people's hearts out. I don't know if she's doing it to look prettier or be stronger or whatever her motivation is. I can't understand it."

Olivia got up from her desk and walked over, putting a hand on my shoulder, "Maybe you need to try. She might not understand Ardetha the way you do, but even if she does there could be a logical reason she feels the way she does."

I waved the idea away. "Knowing her motivations doesn't help the case."

"Maybe not, but it's worth thinking about," Olivia stated as she walked back towards her desk. "While we are thinking about it, let's go meet see if Detectives William and Chang have picked up our sniper."

We had only gotten halfway through the crowded first floor of the police station when I heard a familiar series of sounds that made me stop. Olivia almost crashed into me as I walked backwards a few steps and listened intently. Her gaze followed mine and her jaw dropped slightly. I looked over at her. "Does that video sound familiar to you?"

About a dozen policewomen sat around one of the flat screens which are normally used for a status board. I couldn't see what was on the screen, but the familiar line of cursing and an all to familiar grunt of pain echoed from the speakers. The noises sounded familiar because of the subtle soundtrack of Kansas's *Wayward Son* playing behind the grunts and cursing. I prodded Olivia on the shoulder, shaking her out of her shock enough to get a response. "Are they playing the bar fight from yesterday?"

Olivia was stunned. "I think It's my bodycam footage."

One of the policewomen noticed our gawking and recognized us. She let out a restrained cheer. "There she is! C'mon over here, kid!"

Apparently, Olivia was the focus of this unusual viewing party. I decided to follow along because no matter what happened, I'm certain I could find some method of teasing my partner about it later. The policewoman in question waved at hand at one of her fellows. "Go back to my favorite part!"

Her favorite part was, of course, the moment when Olivia kicked the largest of the Ardetha users right in the testicles. There was an appreciative round of cheer from the circle of women officers. I made a mental note to wear a cup to work, because these ladies were enjoying the moment far too much. One of them handed Olivia a cup of what smelled like soda. "Hey lady. Hope you don't mind us 'reviewing your case', but we heard you took on a whole bar by yourself and had to see it."

I coughed, trying not to sound offended. "She had help."

The officer laughed at me. "Want me to forward the part where you get your ass kicked? This lady took on a whole bar. Haven't seen that since somebody made fun of Samantha Crosse's two year old."

Olivia regained her composure. "For the record, I didn't start that fight. I only managed to hold out more than anything else."

The first officer laughed. "Nobody worth their badge goes around starting fights, but we do appreciate people who finish them."

I couldn't help myself. "Do you guys often watch bodycam feeds?"

"Not unless something really interesting comes up. It's a close-knit department and we've been stealing Chauncey's and Mike's cam footage for years. Chauncey's ability to get his ass kicked and Mike's ability to save said kicked ass is a thing of legends around here. Glad to see you two can do something in that department as well."

Olivia ran a hand over her hair. "Thanks. I think. I'm Olivia, by the way."

The other officer offered her hand. "Officer Homboldt. Agent Black, you mind if we borrow your partner for a bit? We have lady cop things to discuss."

I smiled and consigned my partner to her doom. "I can follow up with the detectives by myself. Just don't run off with her, I might need her to pull my butt out of fight soon enough."

Officer Homboldt looked like she approved. "An excellent choice rookie. I think I saw Williams take Interrogation Room one over a few minutes ago. Now, Olivia, we have a few 'pointers' we'd like to give you on your combat style."

I watched my poor, confused partner being led away and chuckled to myself. I was never going to understand Mhanke Heights. The people of this town were completely unlike the urbanites I had grown up around and were unflappable in the face of adversity. Or at least the giant man-eating lizard kind of adversity.

Chapter 26

Outside the twin doors of Interrogation Room One stood Detective Chang. She was a tall, stocky Asian woman with brooding eyes and a set to her shoulders that spoke of a fighter's instincts. She wore a business suit of pale khaki which looked more at home in an office than a police station. I suspected she probably had at least some close combat training and briefly wondered if any of her videos had ever been cheered over by the policewomen currently gathering around my partner.

She glared up at me and fished a pale cigarette out of her pocket, twirling it in her fingers. She shot me a glare that dared me to mention the anti-smoking ordinance in the building, but I wasn't about to upset two people who had done me a favor. I instead nodded a greeting as I walked up the room. She knocked on the room's blue door and motioned me inside. She explained, "This is your first interview so Williams wants to brief you on your part."

I couldn't help it. "Am I the good cop or the bad cop?"

She rolled her eyes and ushered me into the observation booth. Mhanke Heights may have had a lot of out of date equipment, but the interrogations rooms were well built, with attached observation rooms behind a sheet of one-way tempered glass. Controls sat in one corner for the lone camera looking into the room and an intercom. A computer sat there too, likely for the referencing of case file data. Williams was shifting through papers, assembling a couple folders for the interview from copies he had made.

He glanced up as I went in and offered his hand. "Marcus, Right? How's life in the Weird department?"

"Weird department?"

"Weird department is what we called the ERC when they first opened an office here. You guys deal with most of the weird shit. Not that I haven't had a suspect try to fireball me before, but you guys go looking for such weird crap on purpose. Is this your first interview?"

I nodded. "Outside of staged stuff in the academy."

He grinned and slapped a folder against my chest. "I'm afraid that'll still be true after this one. This is a city case, so I'll be taking the lead and doing most of the actual interviewing. What I need you for is to rile the suspect."

My eyes blinked as I considered the statement. "Rile him?"

He shook a cautionary finger at me. "Not like the movies. Don't go stomping in like a gorilla throwing shit around or anything. I just want you to go in, explain how you located him and you don't find him interesting anymore. As if he was a morning paper you had to fish out of your garden."

I pointed a thumb at the observation window. "How does that help?"

"Hate mongers of every stripe all have one thing in common - they want to matter to the people they harass. If he thinks he can't get to you it'll piss him off and might make him slip up. We have a mostly solid case after the search warrant, but if he slips up and confesses it will be the difference between a dodgy trail and an open and shut plea bargain." His eyes twinkled. "Might even get him to sing about anyone else in this little conspiracy if we get lucky."

I raised an eyebrow. "Fair enough. You'll take over when I'm done?"

WIlliams' face was one of anticipation. "Yeah. Don't bother trying to get a confession out of him - the confession is my job. Instead do what I asked and leave the room because you don't want to waste your time. You are of course welcome to sit in the observation room afterwards."

I held up my hands, palms forward. "You really think we got this guy dead to rights?"

Williams smirked. "I forgot you haven't been updated yet. The moron was literally cleaning the rifle when I broke in. He wiped most the fingerprints, but since my bodycam shows him holding the damn thing it won't do a lick of good. CSI has the rifle now, confirming the ballistics down at the range."

I breathed a sigh of relief. I had been fairly confident in the work Olivia and I had done but hearing it from an experienced officer made all the difference. I gathered myself and took a reign on my emotions. Victor had said the most terrifying thing you could do as a Void-Touched was appear detached. I didn't relish acting out a part rather than doing an actual interview, but if it was what we needed for the case I'd get it done.

Chang took our place in the observation booth as we exited. I took a moment to glance through the folder and nodded at Williams. He nodded and I went in through the grey door of the interrogation room alone.

Cameron Baracus looked like a man better suited to sitting out on his porch and complaining about the weather than assassinating police officers. The man was a study in scruffiness, lean and wiry with hair sticking out in every direction like he had been hit with a jolt of lightening rather than simply cuffed. His shirt was stained and dirty along with his pants and I could not for a moment believe this was the guy who had shot at me. He stared up as I entered and I just stared at him, carefully controlling my facial muscles as to not reveal anything as I sat down. He tried to sneer, but couldn't meet my gaze.

I didn't blame him. It's the lack of pupils which do it. You'd think the fact that my eyes are weird almost-totally black orbs would be what freaks people out, but its the lack of pupils. Humans are used to gauging each other by the body languages expressed in our eyes. To gaze into mine was to be reminded that at least part of me wasn't capable of that form of communication any more. I could be defiant, scared, happy, amused, or any other emotion, and most people couldn't tell but had to hope for context. I didn't give him any context. I didn't show contempt, anger, victory, or any of the other hundred emotions running through my body at the moment. Instead I simply stared at him, saying nothing. I started pawing through the folder.

I'm certain it had all kind of neat pictures in it, but I couldn't tell thanks to my condition. Instead I played the role, roving over them one by one until I hit something I hadn't expected. A page I could read. I smiled then and tried to turn it into one of wry amusement. I don't know how Williams had done it, but there was an honest to goodness page of typed braille on the bottom sheet. I ran my fingers over it and found the talking points

Williams suggested I cover. I hadn't been able to read anything in days, my own personal collection of braille books still in my duffel bag. It was only a few scant notes, but having something to actually read was like rain pouring onto a thirsty man in the middle of a desert. I pulled the paper up and admired it, able to barely make out the tiny bumps in my sight. I had been taught braille early on and could both read it with my sight as well as with my fingers in the traditional manner if the indentations are deep enough. I showed the page to Cameron/ "Braille. I can't read normal paperwork, you know. Not with my condition. This page is the first piece of legible writing I've seen all day."

He attempted to sneer again. "You've got no right to keep me here. I got a lawyer."

"You do," I said, pretending to be more interested in the paper, "not that it'll help. You're a killer, just like the one I was chasing this morning."

"I'm nothing like either of you..."

"Oh shush. You are a murderer, well, an attempted murderer anyway, and all your kind wants to know if how you got caught."

He crossed his arms. "I haven't been caught doing anything other than cleaning a rifle."

"A rifle which was used in a rather crappy attempt to kill a duly appointed officer of the law. Oh and helping a giant lizard escape containment."

He scoffed, but still wouldn't look at my eyes. " I don't know anything about that."

I closed up the folder and went back to the braille paper. "It was the bullet. You probably thought yourself smart by making your own rounds like on the tv shows. The detectives found the kit you used, complete with half-made steel jacketed rounds. The best part is you didn't even need to use those rounds. If you had done 15 minutes of internet research you'd have realized normal rounds would have done the job and been a hell of a lot harder to trace. Of course, thinking is clearly not a strong suit of yours."

He flushed and hammered a finger at the table. "Look here you little..."

I waved him off. "Can it. I know all your opinions already. I've heard them all before from old timers like yourself. All afraid of new things. Afraid of new people."

He made one last attempt for control and attenuated his words with additional jabs at the table. "You. Have. Nothing. On. Me." He growled between clenched teeth. "Plenty of people make custom rounds."

I chuckled. "Great thing we have all your guns then. You understand ballistics is a thing, right? You are partially correct, however. Several people had the right motive and means, but you want to know what led me to you and not them?"

He practically shouted. "What?"

"You're a crappy shot. Everyone else who makes their own rounds and has high powered sniper rifles; they are all ex-military or trained hunters. I don't think you've spent more than a dozen hours shooting your firearm before you used it this morning. Everything you did was rushed and even with a perfect shot at my backside you only nailed me with a ricochet. A ricochet, Cameron. Jesus. You could have nailed me through the car with your *armor piercing rounds a*nd you never made the connection. That is some dumb criminal shit right there. Not only did you screw up the shooting, you actually kept the gun and the ammunition. The other suspects? They all would have killed me and dumped the evidence. Lucky for me it was your dumb butt is the one who actually tried it."

He went from flushed to livid, his pulse pounding close to the surface of his skin. "That's bullshit. You can't make an arrest on something as weak as that! I'll be out in no time you son of a bitch."

I added the paper to the closed folder and waved his objection away. "Nah, we have the guns remember? I have to ask though, why shoot me at all? You never shot at the other IWPs."

"You're a goddamn menace. IWPs should be quarantined, but our corrupt government gave you a badge. That doesn't make you a cop you son of a bitch!"

I sneered. "Actually it does. Along with the four years of education I have on you. Especially the four years of firearm training - I mean, have you actually used a firearm before?"

He lost it and started waving his cuffed hands in the air. "I hit you, didn't I?"

We both froze. The accidental confession hanging in the air like a frigid cloud. We both stared at each other in mute amazement for a moment until Williams waltzed in to break the impasse.

Williams shoot his head while he motioned me out the door. "You know Cameron, I thought we'd have to you present actual evidence to nail your butt, but you just went and blew your wad right there didn't you? Thanks Marcus, I'll let you go now. I'm certain you have more important things to do."

I brightened. I had hoped to rile the suspect up, maybe get him to reveal he was an anti-IWP radical, but I honestly didn't think he'd actually admit to shooting me. Almost made the hospital trip worth it. I waved the paper at Williams. "How'd you know I could read braille? For that matter, where did you get it typed up?"

He smiled. "I called up a friend who has one of them blind typewriters. Didn't want our newest rookie going off track in a recorded session. It makes sense if you couldn't read normal text you must have had some way to study at the academy."

"I appreciate it," I said as I headed out of the room. When the door closed, I quickly ducked in the observation room like a child sneaking into a candy store and pulled up a chair. Detective Chang was writing copious notes on the interview as it proceeded. Cameron hemmed and hawed for a while, trying to deny what had been said, but Williams was a master interrogator and soon drew a more detailed confession out by playing on the man's desire to explain what was wrong about IWPs in positions of authority. It was the usual drivel. Cameron came from the right leaning portion of the antirift-changed crowd, which meant he figured rift changed were all involved in some secret alien conspiracy to control the government, enter their homes and take their freedoms away. This is opposed as to the left-wing anti-rifters nuts, who figured we were too dangerous to be allowed outside of government oversight. Preferably government oversight in a remote prison camp somewhere far away from normal people.

Neither crowd understood the long-term consequences of their short-term solutions. For all the research done in the past decade and half, there still wasn't any know way to stop rifts from happening. Hell, evidence suggested several of the other worlds we knew about were also trying to stop the rifts with technology centuries more advanced than our own and they weren't having any luck either. The rifts and the rift-changed were here to stay. Our numbers were growing too. If our world didn't explode first, some estimated we'd outnumber 'stock' humans in next century or two. What were these nuts going to do when the contained population of rift-changed was greater than the so-called normal population? It was all short-sighted bigotry, just a different shade from the various kinds I'd both encountered and admittedly perpetrated as a gang banger. Bunch of people with no understanding of a subject recommending solutions that hadn't required more than a couple minutes of thought. The void-predator inside me grumbled, looking for a target of our ire. It didn't understand complex thoughts like 'they' or 'those people' and wanted something more tangible to roar at.

I didn't intend to give it one. I congratulated detective Chang on her and her partner's arrest and left to go find my own partner. She was still where I left her, sitting bewildered in a now smaller crowd of women officers, who were discussing the best method of elbow locks.

Yeesh, I thought. How did the men around here not all wear protective padding?

<u>Chapter 27</u>

I got a call from Captain Al-Radke a little while later. He sounded tired, but I suppose we all did. "I heard you found the guy who shot you. Some anti-IWP radical I assume?"

I confirmed it. "Cameron Baracus. He was in trouble for sending threatening letters to rift-changed people a while back. Apparently my coming here tipped the scales in what he considered an 'appropriate response'."

He sighed forlornly. "Remind me to have you two meet some of the nicer people of this town. You only ever get to see the foolish and mean in this line of work."

I smiled, "It's all right boss, Olivia is currently hanging out with half the women of the department."

I could hear a weary grin in his voice. "Us men call them it the 'hen circle'. Don't let the name fool you. They are a support group which likes to go drinking on Tuesday nights and are as likely to start a barroom brawl as they are to finish one. I should tell Officer Jenkins that Olivia would make a decent designated driver. Maybe they'll quit trying to walk home in an unruly mob."

The image of the women I had seen marching down the road with a couple drinks in them was certainly an intimidating notion. "Any luck on the case?"

"No and it's gotten worse. You know the Ardetha patient? The one in the hospital?"

Uh oh, I thought. "...Yes?"

"A friend of hers has gone missing. Detective Stanton gave me a call, she says the parents were describing symptoms similar to the first ones. Sudden weight loss, aggressive behavior. She wasn't reported as having any tell tale signs like changes in her eyes or growing fangs, however."

I nodded, then remembered he couldn't see the motion. "That means she's still in the first few treatments, before the major one. They normally run away right before they get that particular treatment so as to not get sent to the hospital like Abigail was."

He agreed. "Any chance of getting 'Abigail' to talk?"

"I don't think so, she's dead set on finishing her treatments. She won't do anything which would endanger getting the injections."

The captain muttered something unintelligible. "If we can't get to them through the patient, we'll have to try another route. Let's see if we can work our way up from the dealers who will be selling for the gang. Grab detective Williams and see if he has any information on recent changes in drug sales. These guys probably haven't had enough time to establish themselves, which means they are either hiring local dealers or fighting with them for territory. If Williams can't give us a lead, we'll have to look at their established sales territories and see if we can determine where the drugs might be getting stashed. Evidence from the stash could lead us to the hideout."

I didn't know how much help that would be. Unlike most gangs, Ardetha Gangs were often led by smart, educated people recruited by Dr. Partridge himself. They often used multiple locations to keep their various businesses interests separate. Still, we were not generating any leads with Frank Owens or the Beast, so it left us to follow up on the gang in the hopes any single clue to cloud lead to more.

Williams didn't have any more leads as he was still processing the giant stash of evidence and arrests which had come in with breaking up the drug ring Colgate had been a part of. We made small talk for a while as I examined the laminated city map he and detective Chang kept on the wall. "Is this all the known drug activity in town?"

Chang grunted and played with an unsmoked cigarette, which seemed to be an idle habit of hers. "The two of us are the closest thing Mhanke Heights has to a Narcotics department. All the blue pins are called in tips. Red ones are likely true, while the rare green ones are ones we have been able to verify actually happened. Most tips are fellow dealers trying to rat each other out, plus older folks who generally assume any group of three or more teenagers is some kind of drug cabal."

I examined the clusters of pins. The center of the map should have been where Colgate and his friends had operated. "Do you have the gang 's territories marked out?"

"As best as we can determine. Most of these calls don't come with ID or else we'd be able to make an arrest. We have a general idea of what the sales territories are, but they are flexible at best."

I nodded in agreement, gangs didn't always keep strict territory lines unless there was some form of mutual hostility between them. A street corner could hold a dealer from one gang in the morning and anther gang's dealer could operate out of the same corner at night. If business was booming, there might even be opposing gang's dealers on the same street, content enough to tolerate each other in the name of mutual profit. I looked at the map again, annoyed I could only see the pins and not the actual map details. "Could you give me the general rundown on the territories?"

Chang paused for a moment and came up behind me. "I forgot you can't see the marker lines. Can you see the streets?"

I shrugged. "Nope, but I'm fairly certain it's a map of the town."

She wrinkled her nose. "Useful. In 2010 there was only one real gang in town - a splinter group of the Bulldogs who called themselves the Mhanke Heights dogs. About a half dozen older members and a bunch of teenagers. They now operate in the South part of town around here." She indicated an area of the map which was probably close to the apartment buildings we had chased the Ardetha contact out of. "To their east and competing over the newer apartments is the Caberellos. They claim to be part of Santa Muerte, but I'm rather certain that is a bullshit story made up by their leader. When you get out to the docks there a protection racket who oversees some unaffiliated crews that do smuggling and the occasional car theft. The racket is referred to by the misleading name of the 'Night Dockmen'. They dabble in selling, but noone goes over there to buy casual amounts of drugs. The north part of town is generally under the auspices of the Yale street Knives. They recently changed their colors and we think they might be associating themselves with the Bloods for both the reputation and potential business connections. It's standard operating policy for the tinier gangs to sign up under the auspices of a larger one as they grow."

I nodded at her last statement. My crew had started as a few runaways and neighborhood kids working under a high school dropout. Once we got established our leader had eagerly signed up to work under the 486 Bloods, which of course had previously signed up to be part of the greater Bloods organization. These would be complicated business arrangements which were equal parts reputation politics, protection racket, and privileged business transactions. My gaze traveled to the East part of the map, where the convoy check-in point would be, with its affiliated hotels and convoy related businesses. "Who works the convoy area?"

Chang tapped an area just under where I had been looking and where there was a large number of blue pins. "It had been handled by a protection racket called the Dragons. However, most of them haven't been seen recently so I suspect they might have left town or been run off. Your Ardetha gang looks like they are setting up shop there. The Dragons allowed other dealers to operate in their territory for a cut so I'm surprised we haven't seen any violence there yet. The Ardetha covens don't share territory as a general rule."

"You think the Ardetha gang is set up there?"

It was her turn to shrug. "Not for certain. They might be patrolling the area, but they are also popping up around the local high school and junior highs looking for recruits. I recently got a handful or reports of them hanging around the junior college. You think these guys mean to stay?"

I nodded. "I do. I studied these guys in the academy, they like to recruit first before establishing territory. Odds are they decided it was easier to kill or run off the convoy gang to both make an impression and avoid paying any 'import fees'. Once they have enough recruits, a couple veterans will stay behind with most of the recruits while the rest of the gang returns back to their primary site or continues on to another town. With the Beast hunting them down they probably abandoned holding the convoy area, figuring they can take it back later."

Chang cursed and reached for a lighter. "That sounds like a worst-case scenario. If they held the area we might get away with a minimum of violence, but if another gang takes the area over and tries to hold it, there will be blood in the streets when the Ardetha coven takes it back. Do you think the Ardetha coven could do it? They don't seem to be recruiting hardened killers."

"Most gang recruits aren't killers when they join," I pointed out. "In the recruit's case, the Ardetha drug will fast-track them to violence. Between the aggression and the blood drinking, the recruits usually make decent soldier in a couple months."

I contemplated the pins but couldn't draw any helpful conclusions. Even if Chang helped me get context for where each pin was there simply was not a single place on the map where we could pin the gang down. It was possible they had set up near on the schools they were recruiting at, but also as likely to be based somewhere in the convoy area. An exasperated sigh escaped my lips. "We just don't have enough sighting of these guys. I can't figure out for the life of me where they could be hiding. You would thinking someone would notice a bunch of fanged bikers lounging around in public. It's not like they can stay indoors all the time."

Williams looked up from a mound of paperwork on his desk. "What about the missing persons case we sent over? Sarah Tate?"

"She'll be with the gang now, undergoing her final treatments. I'd have to know where their base is to find her."

Williams' face flashed a momentary impatience, the expression of a veteran disappointed by a rookie. "True. Unlike your gang members, Sarah Tate is part of this town. She'll have connections, people she trusted, people who she might have told about the gang. Maybe even people she failed to recruit."

He was right. Abigail hadn't told anyone, but she was a child of a single parent with no major connections beyond a couple other girls in her class. Most her teachers hadn't known anything about the painfully shy girl outside of her name. If Sarah Tate's brief file was any indication, she had also been a shy kid, but a little more connected than her friend Abigail. She had both parents, participating in an after-school activity and was a congregant at a local church. I nodded at the detectives. "You're right. I'm starting to understand how much of this job involves making phone calls."

That earned a sardonic chuckle from Williams. "Just wait until you get to the post-case paperwork. This job can be insanely mundane eighty percent of the time."

So I made more phone calls, alternating brief moments of hope with long dull periods of not getting anywhere. I'm not going to lie to you, on TV the detective shows up at someone's house, gets a critical clue, and whisks off to the next location to save the day. Lucky Bastards. I instead called a pair of grieving parents, struggled to get a dozen teachers to give me details and called another handful of student homes all to turn up little more than some vague descriptions of a generally quiet and purportedly happy girl. It was becoming apparent both girls had been perfect examples of the kind of people who fade into the background, unable to get attention from anyone other than each other. I remembered that feeling before I joined the gang. This missing girl was slowly becoming more personal to me than a mere lead to the Ardetha. It was hard not to feel for her. The final call would be to the Mhanke Heights First Presbyterian Church, a nearby place of worship I had considered visiting on Sunday. I only hoped they wouldn't hold it against me if I asked a bunch of awkward questions now. Before dialing the number, I queried them in our database with my phone. To my surprise, the church had quite the record with Law Enforcement. Apparently, they hosted Wardens on their campus, which meant they had a long history of refusing search warrants and being suspected of hiding fugitives or runaways. I had mixed feelings about their stance. When the rift had first changed me, I had run to a Warden-affiliated church. They had counseled me and hidden me for four days until I decided to turn myself in. The principle of providing sanctuary was an old church custom, but the Warden program made it into a constant source of conflict with the law. Now I was a law enforcement officer, it would be a source of conflict I'd end up in sooner or later. I tried not to think what I would have to do if I had to execute one of those search warrants and instead dialed their number.

An older man picked up the phone. "Bob Herman, First Presbyterian Church, How may I direct your call?"

Apparently, the church had a receptionist. I remembered the name of the head Pastor. "This is Detective Black of the ERC. Is Pastor Kennoch available?"

"Sure, Sure. I'll put him on the line. Hey Pastor!" The man shouted at what sounded like the top of his lungs. "You got the cops on the line!"

There was a pause and another voice came on the line. "Thank you Bob, but next time can you just transfer the call?"

Bob sounded apologetic. "I didn't know if the dumb thing had worked. It's all blinky lights no matter what I do."

The second voice came back. "Fair enough Bob, why don't you hang up and the officer and I can talk?"

Bob seemed to realize he wasn't supposed to be part of the conversation. "Ah, sure Pastor. No Problem." There was a pause, some muffled cursing and a few clicks as Bob figured out how to leave the line.

Pastor Kennoch sounded friendly. "Is that you Mike?"

I raised an eyebrow. I guess any church that hosted wardens would be familiar with the captain of the local ERC department. "I'm afraid not pastor, this is Marcus Black of the ERC. I work for the captain."

If anything, Pastor Kennoch seemed even more excited than before. "Marcus Black! I heard you were coming to Mhanke Heights. You need to come here."

"I intend to on Sunday, pastor."

"No, you don't understand. Sarah Tate is here. I've just called the paramedics and was about to call you."

Chapter 28

I bolted right out of my chair. Olivia noticed my movement and startled. "Sarah Tate is at your church?"

"Yes. She came for sanctuary, but she needs medical attention we can't provide on site."

I juggled the phone while grabbing my gear. "Did she get Ardetha treatments?"

"I think so, but I think the treatments are killing her."

I motioned to Olivia and we ran down to the car.

Olivia drove hard, but without the context clues of street signs to know how close we were getting, I was tense the entire way. The lights of our squad car flashed as we raced down the road. Well, most of them flashed. At least half. We were going to need to take this car in to an electrician before someone got electrouctued.

I looked over at my partner. "Have you ever dealt with Wardens before?"

She shook her head in the negative while her eyes stayed locked onto traffic.

"So they are kind of like volunteer security guards for the church. Officially they ward off vandals and provide help to people who need it outside of the church's operating hours. Unofficially, they'll offer sanctuary to anyone who wants it, hiding them from anyone - even police."

"Does the church have the authority to hide people from the police?"

"No, but since it's private property they can ask us to get a warrant. A lot of the time, the person they are protecting will be smuggled elsewhere while the warrant processes."

Olivia appeared shocked. "That's illegal."

"Not the first time a church has defied governmental laws. We'll just need to be careful. Pastor Kennoch has invited us, but we'll need to be polite or they'll ask us to leave. If we get kicked out it will give them a couple hours to smuggle out Sarah Tate if they feel she's threatened."

She grunted as we turned a corner. "Can I trust you not to do threaten her?"

I winced. "Fair enough. You were right about me and Abigail."

We saw the flash of emergency lights before

we got to the church. The paramedics had beaten us to the scene by a few seconds and I could see them hustling a stretcher inside. Olivia didn't slow down as she approached but instead slid the car next to the church in the kind of drifting stunt best reserved for action movies and car shows. Figuring the screech of tires had more than announced our presence, I stumbled out of the car.

Olivia popped out of the car like nothing had happened and took a moment to straighten her uniform. I decided to keep my trap shut as we mounted the steps. The church was an older building, probably part of the community before the rifts, and was constructed out of worn brick. To our left stood the sanctuary and some connected buildings, probably classrooms, but to our right was another stone and brick building of newer construction. The door was labeled with a cross inside a circle, which I recognized as the symbol of the Wardens, and I mentally noted that the man standing in front was likely the warden on duty. He was wearing a dark color uniform, disturbingly similar to my own, but without any patches or ID beyond a single cross on each shoulder. If it hadn't been the setting, one could have mistaken the man for any of dozens of security guards across the town. I gave the man a nod as we entered. It never hurt to be polite and I did have a soft spot for wardens.

The inside of the warden sanctuary was a large, almost featureless common room with a plastic table and chairs in the center. Three doors on the left contained the office and storage rooms for the wardens, while the three unlabeled doors to the right likely lead to the bedrooms which served people seeking shelter for the night. A man in a collared shirt and sweater kneeled by a young woman I took for Sarah Tate.

I could see why the paramedics had been called. Something had gone terribly wrong with Sarah Tate's treatment. Her head had become asymmetrical, with the right side being taller than the left side. He hair was an almost calico like mix of red, yellow and white hairs. One arm had shriveled and hung loosely at her side, while her feet were bereft of shoes, showing long black talons. There was blood on her clothes, with more leaking from her mouth. A nearby defibrillator lay discarded to the side, showing some emergency first aid had already been required. Her eyes, one the normal green and the other bloodshot to the point of being red, roved everywhere. Her entire body twitched and I noticed with some revulsion that the bones of the shrunken arm were moving beneath the skin.

I had heard Ardetha treatments sometimes go wrong, but this was extreme. Pastor Kennoch stood aside as the paramedics worked to stabilize the patient. We joined him on one side of the room. He briefly waved a greeting to us, but clearly was focused on the drama in the center of the room. His words came out distracted and heavy with worry.

"She collapsed a little after you called. Her changes have slowed, but something it clearly wrong."

The girl continued to shake as the paramedics worked on her. Froth spilled forth from her mouth and they turned her on her sides. The first medic got out an incubator, but Sarah Tate's back abruptly arched at a terrible angle. Her scream was out of breath but full of pain and suffering. There was a terrible cracking sound and she collapsed to the ground. The paramedic checked her pulse and then felt her neck before shaking his head. He gazed sadly over our gathered crowd. "Her spine separated and pushed into her skull. I'm afraid she's gone."

I shuddered. The worst part wasn't seeing her die; the worst was I could still see her body moving, shifting through changes as the Ardetha still struggled to modify a corpse. Olivia turned and vomited on the spot. I wanted to throw up as well, but I instead let my mind run over the logical implications.

"How did she make it here? The gang should have had her contained during the transformation process - it is an important part how they avoid stories like this getting out."

Pastor Kennoch covered the corpse in a blanket. He put his back against the wall and slid to the floor, sitting in a pose of emotional and spiritual exhaustion. "She said one of them tried getting 'handsy' after the treatment was administered. The poor girl panicked and ran for it. Apparently they had trouble catching her. I doubt they would have tried to reacquire her here. Everyone knows Cassius sleeps here during the day."

"Is Cassius the guy outside?"

Gregory Kennoch shook his head in the negative. "We didn't wake him for this. He works the night shift here as a warden. He's an IWP like you, so troublemakers usually steer well clear of the church."

I clenched my fists. "Normally the change is supposed to only take thirty minutes at most and the changes aren't as... uncontrolled as this one was."

The preacher shook his head and put a hand through his balding hair. "It breaks my heart they could put a child through something like that, knowing what could happen, it's unconscionable."

I checked on Olivia, but she waved me off. Instead I pressed the preacher for more information. "Did she say where she had come from? Where the gang was?"

"No, she was having trouble staying focused even before her jaw stopped working properly. She mentioned running between cars, maybe someplace with a parking lot?"

A location with cars didn't help narrow things

down much and brought the worrisome possibility that the gang might be sheltered by a business. I put the thought aside. "Did she say anything else?"

"She talked about Abigail a little. Abigail is a friend of hers. There was three of the girls who were inseparable, but their friend Gina died last year. They both have been really shook up about it."

The paramedics started packing Sarah Tate in a body bag, obscuring the shifting flesh inside. Mercifully, without her heart beating, the changes were slowing to a halt. Olivia steeled herself and started verifying Sarah Tate's identity from the fingerprint reader on her pad. We'd pass the verification along to the coroner once the showed up. With the solemnness of the living amongst the dead, our crowd filed out of the warden building and stood on the church lawn. The Pastor gathered some strength to himself, but his eyes showed the wetness of someone who has lost something precious. He put a hand on my shoulder. "If it's all right with you, I'm going to call her mom."

I nodded absently, still trying to clear the image of Sarah Tate's last moment from my mind. Outside, the day would be shifting into twilight, and while I couldn't see the sun, I took a moment to appreciate the view anyway. Olivia walked beside me and watched the shifting sky with me for a moment. She finally spoke in a tired voice. "I'm sorry about puking back there. The sound… of her..."

I interrupted my partner by placing a hand on her arm. "It's ok. I wish I hadn't been there either. I've known there could be negative side effects with the treatments, but I didn't know that could happen to people. Its not in the files."

She stopped and ran a hand over her face tiredly. "It's late. I think we should call it a night. Hopefully the coroner and CSI team will know more in the morning."

I did some mental math for the distance of the church from my home. I pointed at the car. "Why don't you drive the car home tonight? My place is about a fifteen-minute walk from here and I'll call the captain to update him."

She nodded, likely more grateful she wouldn't have to recount the evening's events to the captain than for a quick trip home. "You okay walking that far?"

I stared at the long rows of streets that made up this area of town. "After what just happened, I need to."

She nodded again and got into the car. I walked along the street, dialing up Captain Al-Radke and updating him on what had occurred. He sighed.

"If we had known about the connection between the girls earlier things might have turned out different. Hopefully the CSI team will find something telling us where she was. In the meantime, get some rest. This team has been worn ragged over these cases and we are all running on fumes. We'll reapproach it in the morning."

I was so tired, I actually nodded before realizing he couldn't see me. Instead I thanked him and wished him a good night as I turned on the main street sidewalk. Part of me didn't want to call it a night. The longer this case took, the more the bodies were piling up. It was abominable enough that the Beast was hunting people, but tonight had been a reminder that the Ardetha gang was just as bloody. It was clear both criminal groups were linked, but not why. The Beast shouldn't know about Frank Owen's life, much less give a damn about it. The question plagued me as I turned on another street, walking up it to my house. I eventually had to admit I was too emotionally and mentally tired to reason anything helpful out. Maybe I'd get lucky and the Beast and the gang would wipe each other out tonight without further civilian causalities. Maybe I'd get my eyesight back and take up a nice career in gym coaching. Both possibilities seemed equally farfetched.

Chapter 29

Fifteen minutes later, I stumbled inside my rental home and stripped off the outer layer of my uniform, including the protective vest. Soon clad in only my boxers and a white t-shirt, I didn't even bother brushing my teeth before crashing onto the inherited bed. Sleep came fitfully for a while, as a stirring in my thoughts brought me to consciousness again and again. I had put my life on the line for this town, for its people, in a near-death struggle. While I had been doing that some of those same people had been spray painting the side of my house with a the demand I leave. I didn't feel like I could blame them too much - as a detective, I hadn't been able to prevent any of the deaths involving the case. It was my first case and the criminals were kicking my ass.

The worst part was the diachroneity. I liked the people of Mhanke Heights, at least on principle. I had sworn an oath to serve and protect them, but had no thanks other than a hastily scrawled graffiti to mark their response. Was the message the work of a few bad apples, or had I found myself in the position of unwanted civic servant?

A voice came from my left, *You should kill them.*

I flipped out of my bed with a start, drawing the pistol. No more sounds came out and I flared my vision. However the hell my eyes worked, they weren't dependent on light and I could see the room as clear as if it was daytime. Nothing moved. I started reaching out to the Other Me when the voice came again.

The neighbor. Kill him too.

Well, that ruled out the voice belonging to my confrontational neighbor. I began to sweep the rooms of the house, one after the other, the pistol held in a rigid firing position.

Find them and kill them all. Challenges cannot be permitted to live.

Holy shit. The voice wasn't coming from outside my head. There was only one being I knew of who thought in such black and white extralegal terms. My 'other half'. Void-predators couched their entire world view in violence and the idea of defeating challenges. I'd spent enough time around my mentor to know that. How the hell was it speaking? It had never spoken before, at most it had offered nudges of emotion whenever violence was a possibility.

You do not answer. Will you kill them?

My voice broke out in the silence. "Hell no!" The sudden verbal outburst reverbated off the walls, making it even more clear how the previous words hadn't existed outside my own head.

The voice, I swear upon heaven, actually sounded petulant. *Why not?* It demanded, like a five-year-old being told it couldn't have ice cream.

"It's not who I am any more. I swore an oath to protect people, not shoot them over stupid disagreements."

It is not a disagreement. They wish to evict you.

"Stupidity is not enough reason to hurt somebody."

A feeling of discontent flooded through me for a moment. *The you I met in the rift would have.*

I tried thinking my response instead of talking out loud like a deranged lunatic. *I'm not that person any more. I'm not going to kill anyone if there's another option.*

There was an actual audible-sounding snort of disgust. I recognized it as the carefully crafted one used by my first year Physical Education instructor. Damn thing was pulling from our shared memories. It had never occurred to me before, but the creature probably had access to my memories from even before we got stuck together. The thought of just how much of my past was known to the thing was chilling.

This is because of the ambush - because you fed. I thought furiously over the implications. Victor had said my parasite, I refused to think of the thing as a symbiote, was immature. If feeding it had allowed it to mature...

I didn't get the thought finished before a wave of will slammed into my own. Muscles tensed as conflicting commands urged them to run and stay. Adrenaline flooded my system, but I held myself fast. I wrestled against the other being inside myself.

There was nothing noble or complicated in our conflict. We slammed our willpower against each other like a pair of elephants fighting over a single doorway. Only one of us could sit in command, and I was not going to let my own personal attack dog decide my actions. Mentally we slammed again and again, until the other presence in my head began to lessen. I didn't let up, forcing it into the tiny space in my head reserved for it. I fell to my knees once its control left and I was in sole control of my body again.

The voice remained. *This is not the way things should be done,* it complained, *The strong should not bend to the weak.*

Too bad, I thought, *this is my way.* When I had

been a teenager I had thought I was strong. I took from those I could and hid from those who were stronger than me. It had been a kind of thinking that promised peace but never delivered, instead it had brought more fear and violence. Realizing that had been a hard lesson which had cost me everything I held dear. This other part of me really was immature - it didn't know better. It was why, I mused, I had to be in control of this ship - even if it was constantly sinking under an ocean of temptation.

I thought about Frank Owens. He didn't appear to be in control either - he wasn't contacting his friends or family, didn't trust law enforcement. Instead he was wandering around town everywhere the monster showed up. I idly wondered what it would be like if the agency tried to track me down if my symbiote ever did take over.

That is when the truth hit me almost like a physical blow. I understood why the Beast was attacking people who knew Frank Owens. I knew the reason because the relation between them was because it wasn't terribly different from the one I shared with my own curse. It was what a symbiote-controlled Marcus Black would do.

All I needed to do was figure out the how.

Chapter 30

By the time Captain Al-Radke and Chauncey came into the office, Olivia and I were already busy going over case notes. She was reading the notes out loud as I hammered her with questions. She was getting a little annoyed at being used as a search engine, but had gotten into it when she realized where we were going. I looked up and nodded at both senior officers as they entered. The captain had his arm in a sling, but otherwise appeared surprisingly fit for duty. Chauncey's appearance was almost prosaic, as if stress couldn't find a hold on him. I noticed his tattoos were glowing again, leaving me to wonder how he recharged so many of the things.

Olivia waved at them. "Marcus thinks he figured out one of our mysteries."

Her bold statement earned a raised eyebrow from the captain. "Which one?"

"I think I know why the beast is attacking people who knew Frank Owens," I stated, motioning Olivia over to the whiteboard. "Could you help me with this?"

She nodded and flipped the board over to its clean side.

I stood up and waved a marker in the air. "Ok. So everyone knows I've got a passenger riding around in my head, right?"

Olivia piped up. "We've decided to call him Murder Puppy."

I sighed. One of us had made the decision and it hadn't been me. I had never thought about naming the Void Predator, but wasn't going to put Olivia out of sorts by complaining overmuch. "Right, back on track. It occurred to me last night that if 'Murder Puppy' was ever in control, he'd probably seek out targets I knew. People I personally disliked or had a grudge against."

Chauncey gave me a strange look. "Why? Wouldn't it just do whatever its instincts tell it? Build a nest, hunt prey, or whatever?"

"Because it's been in my head. It's seen my memories and has experienced the same things I have, or at least has access to memories of experiencing things I have. Over time, my other half has likely stopped seeing those as separate parts from itself and has formed opinions based on my experiences. "

"So other than the scary idea of you on a possessed murder spree, how does it relate to Frank Owens? Are you saying he's in the monster's head like 'Murder Puppy' is in yours?"

I took a moment to pray the nickname didn't stick. "That is what I thought at first, but Olivia and I have going over old case files and found a more likely possibility." I nodded at Olivia and she took over the presentation.

"It comes down to an early case in Russia's ExoReality Investigations Bureau. Peter Harkevich was one of their earliest cases and got caught in a rift event with the FeyWilds, one of the more documented realities the rifts sometimes tie to. It's a huge jungle world with a lot of big and nasty things in it."

She drew a circle on the board with a stick figure in the center of it. "Peter was a unique case. Instead of getting transported over or ending up as one of the rift-changed, he got 'stuck' in a loop with the rift."

At this, she drew another circle with a man in it. The first circle would be labeled 'Earth' and the second 'Feywilds'.

"Long story short, the rift kind of stabilized around him. Instead of appearing and winking out in a few minutes, it would come back exactly where he was every few months. He'd be walking down a road and suddenly be in the FeyWilds. A couple hours of running for his life later, he'd pop back into our world a little bit away. The theory was that he had become connected to something on the other side and they were occasionally swapping places."

The captain looked disturbed. "That breaks a whole lot of rules we know about rifts. They don't stay open and they don't come back. Were they ever able to prove the theory?"

I cut in, "Unfortunately Harkevich didn't come back one day after about 4 years of swapping. The theory was something over there finally killed him or whatever he was linked with. The rift never opened again so it looks like it stayed closed without him around."

The Captain nodded. "Fair Enough, but what does this have to do with our Person of Interest?"

Olivia brightened, clearly excited to be talking about something she found personally interesting. "Harkevich claimed he would dream about being a prey animal in the FeyWIlds, he stated he remembered sights, sounds and memories of another existence over there. It was generally assumed it was a side effect of his psyche adapting to the constant danger he was in, but what if it wasn't?"

I interrupted, "What if Frank Owens and the Beast are swapping? We never see the beast move around because he's Frank Owens when not on the hunt. We weren't looking for him on the camera feeds, only the beast. Later, when he attacks a target, he's the Beast and we never see Frank Owens. We've kind of assumed Frank didn't make it, so we haven't made the connection."

Mike was still skeptical. "It's a decent theory, but why would it be going after his business associates?"

It was Chauncey who picked up our train of thought. "Frank Owens avoided joining a convoy because he was smuggling for the gang. The smuggling side-job was why he was out there on the road when the rift occurred. He can't do anything about the Beast or his own involvement because they are one and the same. Worse, he might not even blame either for the accident."

The captain threw up a confused hand, "So the apartment was, what? Frank Owens attacking his own apartment?"

I shook my head. "Olivia and I checked with CSI. They found blood at the scene, but didn't fast track the ID because there was no body. I think the gang sent someone to retrieve the drugs and they got caught in the act by Frank Owens. They made their way out of there, and the damage caused by the beast covered up their presence."

Mike nodded his head slowly. "It would clear a few things up. So you are saying the Beast is being affected by Owen's mental state? Since it can't understand the complexity of his emotions, it's killing those people Frank Owens blames. Why hasn't he come forward? Helping people caught in events are our jurisdiction, after all."

I stared down at my hands for a moment. "You are assuming he doesn't want the killings. What if he's happy with the Beast's actions? What if this is his way of getting revenge in everyone he blames for his wife's death? He may even be feeding the Beast memories and emotions to keep it going."

Mike's eyes opened wide. "May Allah preserve me. You are talking about a human serial killer with a giant monster at his beck and call." He took a moment and contemplated the implications. "It's a good theory. We'll use it for direction until something proves it wrong or right. It means the gang will be the first target, but other townspeople may targeted be after that. Hell, we are probably the next targets given how many times we've shot at the Beast. No one is leaving the building without their partner."

For someone with one useable arm and probably a decent number of painkillers in his system, Mike Al-Radke was fearless under pressure. He looked over at his partner, "Chauncey, you are going to call up everyone we interviewed about Frank Owens. Find out if he had any other grudges. I'm going to review the camera feeds to see if we can verify Frank Owens was the one walking around after the fence was penetrated. Catching him going to the warehouse will help verify the 'swapping' theory."

He looked over at me, but before he could say anything, I interrupted him. "I'd like to visit Abigail Smithson again."

All the faces present turned to me. Captain Al-Radke raised an eyebrow. "Are you certain? Your last interview didn't go so well, I hear."

I blew out a breath. "We need to know where the gang is. I think I can get her to open up to me."

Al-Radke turned to Olivia. "You're his partner. Do you think he can do it?"

Olivia looked me straight in the eyes. "I think he can."

<u>Chapter 31</u>

We arrived at the hospital an hour later. Because my luck always seeks to put me in the most dangerous situations possible, Bambi had just come on shift. I received a glare capable of stripping paint and the quiet, growly admonition that making Abigail cry again would result in a terrible amount of physical discomfort. I tried to be blaise about the threat, but it was hard considering this was a woman apparently scared Chauncey, who I now knew was a walking spell-assisted tank. I figured jumping out the window and trying to land on my feet would probably be a safer solution if it came down to it.

Abigail was still in the same room I had left her in. Her eyes were puffy and swollen from crying, she must have heard us enter but didn't look up. I couldn't blame her. Remembering Olivia's advice, I decided to start with a gentle approach. I sat down in one of the plastic chairs the room had been provided with. I said, "I'm guessing you heard about Sarah. I'm sorry for your loss."

She words came out bitter and strained, but I didn't blame her. "You going to tell me how I could have prevented it if I had told you?"

I shook my head. "No. That wouldn't be true"

"It is exactly what Mrs. Tate said. She's right."

I leaned back. "I'd have to disagree with Mrs. Tate. Look kid, did you know I used to be in a gang?"

That got her to life her head. "But you're a cop."

"Wasn't born a cop. I was born to a single mom with 5 kids and no way to pay the rent most months. Our home was crowded and stressful. You probably don't know about poor and crowded, but I think you know what it's like to feel freer when you're outside your home than when you are inside it."

She didn't say anything. I had read her file. She was the only child of two work-aholic parents. The kid had access to money and safety, but I was gambling, like me, she hadn't had the attention or support she'd needed growing up despite having all the 'well-adjusted' kid checkboxes checked. Apparently, a parent who isn't home is just as negative as a missing one, regardless of whether they are working or in jail. I pressed on.

"I had a couple friends in junior high. We all stuck together because we were never going to be the rich kids or the popular kids or even those dramatic types who all have something in common. The only time someone paid attention to us was when we got in trouble. I guess all the teachers figured we were too normal to worry about and not exceptional enough to care about."

She shrugged. I'd hit a nerve.

I looked out the window. "I suppose a lot of kids feel that way in junior high. The important part to this story is there was this guy in our neighborhood who didn't overlook us. His real name was Dean, but we called him 'Wheels'. It was a nickname because he had a weakness for stealing fancy cars, the kind you aren't supposed to boost. He'd run them all over town and leave them someplace random so the police wouldn't figure out it was him. He liked us, used to talk to us when we went by his place, gave us rides when we needed it. He even provided a place to sleep if home got too crazy. There were several of us kids who looked up to him because he was such a kind guy. After a while, we started living with him. By the time I was 16, we were part of the 486 Bloods. One of their better car and property theft crews. We'd grab what we could, Dean would fence it through the Bloods and we'd all get drunk on both success and liquor."

Abigail shrugged. "I didn't want to join because someone was nice to me."

This was uncomfortable territory for me. Whatever my confession to Olivia, I was naturally terrified about discussing my past. The whole point of starting a new life is supposed to be leaving the old one behind, but I needed those memories now. I needed to talk about my reflections on them to someone who I thought might have come to similar conclusions, given enough time. "I didn't join the crew because Dean was nice to me. I joined because he said I was special. Being special to someone was what I wanted, really. I think you can relate to wanting someone out there to care about you more than a random stranger. Once I was in, I became the most dedicated car thief the 486 had ever known. I drank it in when they called me the 'Getaway man', when they offered to teach me things people outside the crew didn't know. I would have done anything to be special and for years I did."

Abigail tried to study the empty space beyond me. "You going to tell me the special is inside me all along? That if I smile more, I'll have more friends and boys will want me?"

I snorted. "No. I'm going to tell you something worse. I'm as unique as they come. IWPs are less than 1% of the population and Void Touched are rare for IWPs. No, I'm going to tell you that you can be the most special person in the world and it still just as terrifying to talk to people."

I paused searching for the words. "Look. You've lost two best friends and not many people have been in to listen to you."

She stammered for a moment, thrown off balance. "Just Pastor Kennoch, but..."

I nodded. "I understand. No one wants to tell the preacher about how they are feeling un-Christian. You can tell me about the gang or not. It's not the question I wanted to ask."

That got me a confused expression from both Abigail and Olivia. I continued, "I told you why I joined the 486 Bloods. I'm not going to pretend I know why you joined the coven, but I think I might be able to understand if you explained it to me."

Abigail stared at me for a long moment. "You really want to know?"

"Sure," I said.

"No one else wants to. The pastor wants me to stop. My parents don't give a shit what happens to me. Most other people have their own damn opinions about what I'm doing. Even you."

I couldn't deny the truth so I opened my arms to the accusation. "You're right, but Olivia here," I motioned towards my partner, "is also right. I only have a theory. You have the truth. The real truth. I'm a cop, so the truth is what I should want, right? Even if it doesn't match my theory."

The kid looked towards Olivia with new-found respect. "Fine, but no interruptions, no questions. Got it?"

My partner and I chimed in together. "Got it."

She sighed. "My parents work late most nights. Hell, the work late most weekends too. I'm not certain why the hell they choose to have a kid. It sure as hell wasn't to spend time with me. Instead, I eat food I make myself, sit in an empty house and worry if I'll see anyone I'm related to before I get up in the morning. School was better but it was really just the three of us. That was my whole world. I'd only get up in the morning so I could hang out with Sarah and Gina. They had crappy homes too and they understood what is was like not to want to come home. We'd hang out long after school, just walking around downtown, you know? Life was crap, but I had friends, so it wasn't total crap."

She sniffled for a little while and I let her. It was almost painful to not speak up, but silence was what I had agreed to.

"It happened when we were walking one night and some of those gang bangers from south side came by. They wanted us to get in their car, but we weren't going to do it. They thought we were cruiser chicks but we were just walking, you know? They should have left us alone. They weren't listening to us saying no and Gina finally lost it. She chewed them out big time, cussing and everything. The big one, he was this older dude. He reaches over the door of the car, grabs her and casually bashes her head against the car. She's bleeding and we are yelling for help and he does it again. She's still alive. She's screaming for help and that was when the car takes off. She was still alive when she fell under the car."

I couldn't help it; the word comes out in a whisper. "Jesus"

"We tried to ID them later, but nothing ever came out of it. I saw Gina's body, or what was left of her and all the police could say was 'sorry'. Sarah and I, we realized something that day. We were weak. Anyone could come any time and take whatever they wanted from us. Even our lives. Nobody would protect us, no one would care. Hell, most wouldn't even attend our funerals - they sure as hell didn't attend Gina's. That asshole and his car changed everything. Now I know the world isn't safe like the adults say it is."

She looked over at me. "That was why I need the treatments. With the Ardetha I'll be stronger, tougher, untouchable. If someone tries to hurt us, we'll be able to hurt them instead. Power is what I want the treatments for. I don't want to hurt anyone, but I'll do it to protect myself. "

She sighed and the teenager suddenly looked much older, world weary and broken. She looked straight into my eyes and my heart broke a little. No kid should ever look like she did right then. "I thought the coven would protect us and in return we'd help protect them. That wasn't how it happened did it? They didn't protect Sarah. They killed her and might have killed me too screwing around with their formula."

She lowered her head and wept for a while. After a while she wiped her eyes and clenched a fist. "I won't protect them."

This was a delicate moment. The right words might get us everything, the wrong ones might get us nothing. Well not nothing, I realized; Olivia had been proven right. I had been completely wrong about Abigail's motivations. "Protecting each other was part of being in the 486, but it wasn't why I joined. You were right Abigail. I was wrong about your motives. I guess I can understand why you might want to be safer, even if I don't agree with the method."

The kid's eyebrows raised, and she slowly nodded. "Thanks. I don't need you to agree with me, but I wanted people to understand why. You think the pastor would listen?"

I shrugged. "I don't know him very well, but its pretty clear he cared about the two of you. It is his job to listen and not judge right?"

She snorted. "Supposed and Does are two different words. Listen, I said I wouldn't protect those bastards and I meant it. I've never seen their hideout, but I'm pretty certain I know where it is."

Tears fell from her eyes, but there I could see

the cold steel behind them. "Mr. Hernandez. He owns a recycling yard out by the convoy area. He's also the coven's local contact. John said Hernandez was his recruiter."

It was more than I could have hoped for. A recycling yard would be a perfect place to hide a dozen bikers and their gear. The vast expanse would mean a lot of noise would be muted for the neighbors and most could be chocked up to the yard's day to day operations. The business would also have hidden the movements and smuggling actions of the gang under legitimate salvage and metal trading. I looked over to Olivia and then back at Abigail. "Thank you Abigail."

She hadn't let up her cold gaze. "Don't thank me. Just promise me you find out which one fucked up Sarah's treatment. You jail his ass. Nobody got justice for Gina, but someone needs to get justice for Sarah. I need to know at least one of them did."

Olivia and I rose. I rubbed the badge on my chest absently. "I promise, Abigail. We won't rest until we find them and arrest them."

Chapter 32

It sounded heroic, but it wasn't a promise I knew if I could keep. We headed out from there and called the Captain from the car. As soon as he picked up I rushed out the words, "Mr. Hernandez, business owner of a recycling yard."

"John Hernandez. I know him. Are you certain of this information?"

"Abigail told us. He's the gang's local man."

"Excellent work Marcus. Get your butt over here on the double, I'll get some backup for us and we'll hit them tonight. "

A smile escaped my lips. We finally had the information we needed and tonight at least one of the town's monsters would be put to rest. It would be dangerous, but damn it felt great to be moving forward.

The Captain made the arrangements over the next couple hours. Patrol officers set up a stakeout across the street who verified that, in addition to the half dozen of John's usual employees, several other biker types could be seen entering and leaving the compound at all hours. The local SWAT detachment, which was headed up by none other than Officer Homboldt, was deployed a couple blocks away in their APC, ready to roll up on his word. I probably shouldn't have been surprised to find out the aggressive officer was their sergeant. The plan was simple, patrol officers would post a couple cars along the borders of the yard while the SWAT team waited in their APC. Our ERC team in its entirety would scout the yard and discover which building held the gang's operation. We'd engage if necessary, but hopefully hold position until SWAT arrived with their vastly superior firepower. Mike directed us to a piece of fence line along the back of the property, close to where it bordered the town safety fence. The location surprised me.

"Why don't we simply come in the front and execute the warrant?"

Mike shook his head. "This place is supposed to be their location of last defense. They'll have the entrance covered and are more likely to shoot than answer questions. The patrol officers will cover the entrance once the action starts. We just need to locate them for the APC."

Chauncey came up holding a large roll of paper. "You rookies will appreciate this. The fence is likely warded to detect any breaks in itself. It's risky to cut it."

He unrolled the paper and I saw the surface had been covered in a larger version of a tattoo glyph, written out in what I assumed was a mana conductive ink. A plastic and metal control chip was glued to the bottom. I looked at him askance. "Will that work?"

He chuckled and started taping the paper to the fence using scotch tape. "Yeah. I can teach it to you if you want. I'm guessing the academy hasn't taught any classes on it yet, but this is how we test tattoo designs before inking them permanently. It's safer if the paper explodes instead of your arm."

My eyebrows rose. "Is the paper exploding a possibility?"

He clucked at me. "Probably not, but then again I did draw it while sleep deprived. You might want to stand back." Chauncey pulled a tiny mana battery out of pocket by two short wires he had soldered to the ends. He taped one wire to one line and held the other end over another line of the intricate glyph. He looked over at the rest of the team. "Once I connect this lead, run through the paper as fast as you can. I'm not a hundred percent certain of how long the charge will last once I activate the glyph. You really, really don't want to be passing through when the battery runs out."

With that cheery note of caution, he added another piece of tape to the loose wire and slapped it against its designated line. There was a flash of activation and the paper along with the fence behind it became translucent. A phase spell, I realized. It was some pretty complex magic to come up with in a couple hours. I would have loved to have taken time to admire it, but Chauncey's warning was ringing in the back of my head and I plunged in after Olivia as we went through the translucent image of the paper.

We passed right through the fence as if it wasn't there. Mike and Chauncey followed a while later and we split into two teams without even looking back to see if the phase spell was still in place. Olivia and I took the right path at a stack of partially crushed cars and I let her take the lead. It might not sound chivalrous, be we had agreed she was more likely to survive a sudden outbreak of enemy fire, while I could cover the rear better with my sight. I mentally unbarred some of my mental reserves holding the void spirit inside of me back and it was practically dancing with anticipation of the hunt. Void predators were made for this kind of situation and its instincts flowed through me, helping me recognize dangerous corners and potential blind spots. I also felt the energy of the void eagerly flow into my limbs, but held back on letting it get too far. I didn't want to risk a control problem during this sensitive portion of the assignment. Twilight had faded to night, but the lights scattered throughout the compound gave the team illumination as we pressed forward.

I could feel my own anticipation building up

inside of me as I turned a corner. If we could close the noose on the Ardetha gang and take them out of the picture, the Beast and Frank Owens would have no choice but to deal with us to get to them. We could finally put an end to the violence and get the justice the town had been denied for so long.

It didn't take us long to figure out that the gang wasn't in the primary business office or large work area. Several bikes were stacked up against a wall, but apparently they knew better than to hang out where the general public could see them. We instead started maneuvering closer to the larger storage sheds in the center of the yard. I followed my partner through another corner and were almost in sight of the first shed when the deep throated sound of a shotgun roared out and Olivia was flung back, landing near my feet. I felt an errant pellet zip by my cheek and dropped to a knee as my training took over. The shotgun holder leaned out to see what his shot had done and I loosed a round towards his head. I only managed to draw a line across his scalp, but he yelped and dropped the shotgun as the round grazed him. He attempted to reach for his weapon, and I put a bullet through his forearm. I could hear additional shots ring out to my left and knew the rest of the team was engaged as well. The com piece in my ear chattered as Captain Al-Radke notified the SWAT team of our position and the incoming fire. I checked Olivia and pulled her further back as she struggled to her feet. I could see dents in her flesh where the pellets had entered, but she didn't appear hurt over all. If anything, she only seemed annoyed.

I was radioing in our position when additional fire opened up on our flank. Olivia had recovered from her initial shock and we attempted to cover each other as we walked backwards towards the sounds of Chauncey and Mike's own firefight. I had been in shooting battles before, but a person never gets used to the nature of a real, random firefight. There's this terrifying sensation which comes with knowing you won't be able to see the round that kills you. Your mind tries to track where the fire is coming from, but once you see the flash, it is already outdated information. The not-knowing creates a sense of pervading fear and adrenaline which has no equal. I would rather face any of the ugly monsters I've come across in my career than engage in another open firefight. I hadn't been in many firefights, but I'd learned the best thing to do was shove all of the fear aside and concentrate on the parts you can affect, usually returning fire and hugging cover.

Olivia may have been unused to live combat, but she reacted as smoothly as she had in the initial ambush. We traded turns firing and falling back, relying on the cadences carefully drilled into us by the academy. For a moment I thought we were doing well, but then a bullet zipped by my head coming from behind. I put out an arm to halt Olivia as we tried to compensate for the most recent direction of fire. I could see Chauncey and Mike in the near distance, but the gang had set up a third field of fire between the stacks of junk we were using for cover.

Things looked pretty bleak when there was a sudden boom behind the northernmost gang member's line. The SWAT Apc, a military surplus M113 dubiously named 'Rhino' suddenly plowed through a stack of washing machines. Someone had welded a ramming bar across the front with a picture of the African mammal stenciled on the front. Armored SWAT team members spilled out the rear of the thing and total chaos erupted as the sides were suddenly matched. There was a zooming flash of light and the APC rocked back on its tracks as glowing fire spread against it in a punishing arc. Great. They had their own mage. Of course they did. Genetically modified vampire super soldiers weren't enough, one of them had managed to pay for his own set of spell tattoos. The APC driver jumped out of the vehicle right before a second flash penetrated the thin aluminum armor and set the insides aflame.

I cursed. A mage could be a major problem, even if they probably only had a few spell tattoos. There was always the chance one of them had actually memorized all the instructions necessary to cast on their own. It they were that good it meant they wouldn't have to worry about running out of spells to toss at us. We still had the edge of numbers, but the gang just needed the opportunity to close the distance in order to change things in their favor.

Olivia nudged me with her elbow. "How many clips do you have left?"

I did some mental math. I had brought 10 with me but had been spending bullets like I had brought a hundred. "6 spares and the half in my pistol. You?"

"Little more than that. Mag Quickloaders are expensive but you can pack a lot of them in a pouch."

I'm guessing the SWAT team members probably had slightly more ammunition, but their shotguns and SMGs wouldn't last forever. I swept the area with my sight and examined the glowing pinpricks of human souls. My vision confirmed, at least for the moment, we had pinned the suspects down. To my surprise there appeared three more points at the edge of my vision. They were moving way faster than anyone could run and I realized what I was seeing a heartbeat later. I shouted into my headpiece. "Bikes! We have three bikes incoming from the west, maybe more!"

Homboldt's SWAT Team didn't say a word, just smoothly reoriented into an adjusted formation which had three of them facing our rear. The shift put Olivia and me on the far right flank and I tried to watch both the incoming flankers and the firing enemies at the same time. To my surprise the bikes slowed down and stopped a couple hundred yards out, right before crossing into a normal line of sight. The roar of their engines was audible now and I could see at least two more bikes come up behind them. There was more of these guys than I had thought. The firing from the front died down and there was an eerie silence in which the only audible sound was the thrum of the bike engines and the post-firing ringing in our ears. A man walked up casually behind an overturned refrigerator. He didn't have the vein tattoo motif of the coven, but his red eyes showed at least some Ardetha treatments had been performed on him. He tried to appear unimpressed, but I noticed he kept close to the refrigerator in case he needed to duck for cover.

The man opened his mouth to speak, but Mike beat him to it. "I've got a warrant for your arrest John Hernandez. Along with several of your friends there."

John Hernandez looked unphased. "I don't think you brought enough cops for that Mike. I think if you and your friends agree to leave here now, I could find my way down to the office tomorrow morning."

His offer was a complete bluff. John knew he couldn't keep operating now the police had performed a raid. The best he could hope for was that we would give him and his new friends enough time to evacuate to another location or skip town. He would have the upper hand for the moment, but we could call in far more officers than he could call in additional gang members. Mike countered the offer. "Why don't you all surrender now, and I guarantee a fair trial and protection from a certain giant predator beast who has it in for you?"

John got pissed and pointed his shotgun over at Mike's location. "That is bullshit. I gave you..."

He never got to complete the sentence. As soon as his shotgun pointed at our positions, Chauncey had popped out and released a blue bolt of spell energy at the scrapyard owner. He went rigid and the firearm discharged, hitting one of the makeshift barricades. The shotgun wielding thug's muscles spasmed and I realized I was looking at some kind of long-range version of the taser spell Olivia had. There was a moment of silence as everyone watched the gang boss topple over into the dirt, continuing to twitch. Even the SWAT officers were looking surprised, amazed that Hernandez had actually put himself out there and Chauncey had actually nailed the bastard. Someone gave a loud whoop and was answered by the boom of a shotgun discharge. The firing took up again. I turned towards the bikes and managed to squeeze out a couple rounds aimed at the large machines as they turned towards us. Luck had me nailing the front tires of one machine, and it tumbled into the dust, spilling the unlucky biker right into the dirt. Pain exploded in my chest as an answering round hit me nearly dead center. My bulletproof vest took the shot right in one of the ballistic plates, but I still fell over from the kinetic impact. I saw Olivia dropping prone next to me as more shots passed over her head. She picked her headpiece out of the dirt and yelled into it. "Jack in the Box!"

That had been our word for a perimeter breach. It meant that things would soon move to hand to hand and the Ardetha vampires would have the upper hand. The only thing stopping them from running everyone over is a blood maddened rush would be Olivia, Chauncey and myself. Our 'abilities' may not mean much against firearms at range, but in an all-out brawl it was pure monster versus monster.

The voice came up to my mind, hissing with excitement. *You promised. Let us kill these challengers!* I nodded and reached inside of me for the power waiting there. The void-stuff flooded into my chest and out to my limbs. Our shape began to blur at the edges and gain shadows which fell from no discernible source. Our finger lengthened to talons as a double-row of fangs push from the flesh of our jaw. We felt the exultation of the challenge as the first biker attempted to drive past our position. *We* were one; we were the hunter unleashed.

There wasn't any time to think. Instead we leapt in front of the bike as it zipped past. The collision sent the bike, it's driver and ourself right into a jumbled heap that skidded a decent 50 feet. By the time it had ended, our claws had driven into the man's chest and left him disabled with a collapsed lung. We had taken some muscle damage in the blow, but it mattered little as another one of the gang members slammed us against a pile of steel boxes. Each blow was far stronger than the ones we could give and only strong training and a little bit of the void-stuff in our limbs managed to deflect most of the blows aimed at our abdomen. In desperation we headed butted the vampire and the modified human stumbled back, opening room. This one's eyes were still human-looking, meaning they were probably an older version of the Ardetha treated. The gang member clearly had some experience with this kind of thing because he hunched down like a boxer and came at us again. Remembering the ERC Academy training, we sidestepped the rush and threw a blow right at the man's temple. Marcus curled the fingers at the last moment, causing the target to be knocked unconscious instead of killed on the spot. The void-spirit grumbled at the lack of killing, but the agreement had been to reduce casualties if possible. Luckily the next assailant had a firearm which meant all bets were off as we lashed out at his chest at full extension. Instead of piercing the target's chest, our partially-real talons sunk deep in and grabbed at the fragile anchors that bound soul to flesh. The prey only had a moment to scream in agony before the connection was broken and his body fell limp in a mask of agony. Like all the flesh beings, the demise of his soul left a husk of flesh with no animation save a twisted expression of pain and fear. There wasn't time to glory in the kill, but we drank the gathered energy in as we searched for the next victim. The sight of the prey's soul fading into whatever waited beyond was in the corner of our eye as we jumped onto the pile of steel boxes. Part of us screamed and railed against the killing, but not so loudly that we didn't continue the fight.

The conflict had turned into a melee. The SWAT team hadn't been as outmatched as we had feared and was working in tightly knit pairs, using shock batons and pistols to duel the vampires and their improvised clubs and blades. One of the officers dropped to the ground as a blade cut their hamstring. The open space provided an opportunity and we leapt at the attacker, catching them unawares and driving claws deep into their right chest. We must have collapsed a lung, but the injury failed to slow down the vampire, who probably didn't even understand why theit breathing had become difficult. Instead, the Ardetha vampire turned a pair of red eyes towards us and delivered a backhand which sent our body flying towards a pile of rusted cars. We phased into the void slightly, cushioning the blow, but delaying our rise as we carefully disengaged from the rubble. The SWAT officers hadn't hesitated and had turned our distraction into a finishing blow by both applying their stun batons to the target at the same time. Marcus mentally noted that using two different taser sources was potentially lethal and the void-spirit hoped it was. Sure enough, the twin alternating currents stopped the target's heart and his anchors began to decay. Moving closer let us feed off the energies of the cooling corpse as we checked the officers over. It was the pause that let us properly see the washing machine flying at our face.

It hadn't occurred to us just how strong the Ardetha vampires were until the washing machine flew at our face. There was no point in trying to deflect the thing, so we dropped to the earth as it sailed overhead, missing the top of our falling head by inches. John Hernandez strode into the fray, one fist covered in blood and the other clenching a ragged scrap of iron. Chauncey intercepted him. Most of the officer's tattoos had gone dark from use, but he was still able to deliver a telekinetic blow which threw Hernandez to the side.

John Hernandez didn't so much as cry out as he hit a rusted-out car shell. The man was like something out of one of those terminator movies. He kept walking forward after each invisible blow from Chauncey. Our blood ran cold and we let Marcus come to the fore to evaluate the threat. Ardetha recruits are often out of shape before their treatments, but John Hernandez had been a hard-working street tough in the peak of his physical condition when he'd started injecting the drug. Even without the full set of treatments, he was likely one of the strongest opponents in the ground. He eventually managed to gain enough ground to swing a low kick at Chauncey. Chauncey dodged, but lost track of the calculations needed for another spell. Hernandez didn't hesitate but instead launched into a full set of blows and counterblows designed to prevent the mage from recovering. Chauncey knew he wasn't going to survive the onslaught and hissed a single word, activating one of his few remaining tattoos. There was a sudden lack of solidity to his form which hadn't been there before and he slid through his opponents attacks as if the man wasn't really there. The void spirit provided the answer, *He fades, like us. Can other flesh-things fade?*

We filed the question away for later. Before John Hernandez could recover from his surprise and realize Chauncey was behind him, we came in to his side, ripping with our claws. Deep gashes were opened in the man's skin, but he slammed his arm back at us like a postal worker might throw off a rabid dog. Determined not to open the fighting distance, we held onto the limb and tried to drag Hernandez down to the ground. We might as well have been pulling on a construction crane. Hernandez punched his with the other arm; once, twice, and there was a cracking of ribs under the blow. We countered by stomping down on his lower leg. It twisted and there was a howl of pain and rage. Hernandez went completely into the attack, swinging with both arms as quickly as he could, less interested in where he was striking as he was in satisfying the deep need for bloodlust in his soul. We tried blocking the blows and even cutting his arms as we could, but the vampire's strength was much greater than our own. A powerful kick knocked us to the ground and we rolled to avoid a hammering stomp.

Things were bleak. We were out of options and there wasn't time to call for help. We tried to get up, but a hammering blow to out midsection sent us sprawling back. John Hernandez loomed over us and we prepared to receive a final blow.

Chapter 33

Salvation came in the form of a random bullet. It slammed into John Hernandez's shoulder and knocked him to the ground like a giant hammer and swung into his side. There was a stunned moment of disbelief as we processed the sudden change in position than the panicking excitement in knowing we were alive but only had moments to keep it that way. We got up onto a knee and slammed a fist into John Hernandez as he struggled upwards. Chauncey came to my aid and pulled out a pair of steel handcuffs, sticking John Hernandez's wrists together and hopefully reducing his threat in the current conflict. I took the opportunity to gaze around at the developing melee. Several SWAT officers were down, but the gang only had a few members up and moving. For a brief moment we began to relax and I could feel our identities starting to separate again.

I shouldn't have let down my guard. It was a rookie mistake and Chauncey paid for it. Chauncey had been finishing cuffing John Hernandez when a line of bullets suddenly started in front of the suspect and stitched up his torso, nailing the kneeling Chauncey several times in the chest and arm. The two shot men fell backwards and I stood there frozen for a moment. My gaze lifted up to see the form of a man kneeling on top of one of the stacks of junk. He could not have looked less likely a sniper if he'd tried. He wore a polo shirt and torn khakis, looking more like a casual tourist than a murderer. His hair was a weird tangle of frizzed ends and you would have wanted to ask if he was lost except for his eyes. Those weren't sane eyes. They were wild and paranoid eyes, unable to stay in any once place or focus on any one thing for long. Despite the constant movement there was an intensity in them that can't be matched by anyone who still believes in reality. I had never laid eyes on him before, but I knew this had to be Frank Owens.

I scrambled for my pistol, still thankfully clamped in its holster. Aiming it in Frank Owens direction, I tried to see if I could talk him out of what I suspected could end up as a massacre. If my theory about him was correct, we could be dealing with the Beast at any moment. I tried to speak in a placating voice, but didn't drop the point of my gun away from his chest. "Hello Mr. Owens. Come to see the coven arrested?"

He smiled like we had shared a fantastic joke. "Oh no, officer. I've come to end it. End it all."

I saw a swat officer slowly make her way towards Chauncey out of the corner of my eye. I waved my free hand to keep Frank Owen's attention. "That seems a little drastic. I understand you have a condition we could help you with."

He cackled and crawled down the stack. Crawled on all fours like some kind of human spider. I still don't know how he managed to not slip and tumble down the pile of metal junk the hard way. It massively magnified the creep factor. His grin continued. "What if I don't want my 'condition' helped?"

I wanted to back up and open more space between us, but if I couldn't talk him down I would need to be close to grab the gun. I shuffled a half step closer instead and spoke as carefully as I could. "C'mon Owens, I know about the switching. Every time that thing comes over here it leaves you in a place so dangerous we've only ever heard about it from secondhand accounts. I don't know how you've survived this long, but you can't expect to last much longer in the FeyWilds."

The revelation gave him pause and he settled on his haunches astride the remains of a Toyota corolla. "It's a strange feeling you know? Running and hiding for your life in one place and still be here, delivering justice."

Wow, I thought, you really can distract the villain by getting them to talk about themselves. I decided to double down on the cliché. "What justice, Frank? John Waters was nothing more than a kid and you bit his head off. He wasn't responsible for what happened to you."

"Wasn't he?" Bitterness mixed with the madness in Frank Owens' voice and I felt the tension eking out between his teeth. "They wanted their stupid drugs, so I agreed to run them. Outside the convoys. I needed the money and they knew it. Always acting superior, never telling the truth about what could happen out there. They are to blame for her death, not me."

I saw a flash of movement and noticed Olivia sneaking up behind the stack of junked cars Frank Owens was perched on. I agreed with the motion, talking to Frank Owens was buying us time, but I wasn't going to be able to talk him back to rational thinking. "Are they? You could have turned down the offer Frank, told them you'd do it another day."

He spat, "Don't you get it? They brought me here. Brought me to the car and the pain and the world with alien trees and square buildings."

Uh oh. That didn't sound like Frank Owens memories or opinions, I thought. The mixing of the two mentally might have been more complicated than I had initially realized. I shuffled another half-step forward and shook my head. "What do you mean Frank? You were born here. It was your car."

"No!" he shouted with a roar. "It wasn't my car. Not my fault! They did it. They made me drive, made me kill!"

Something clicked into place in my head.

Frank Owens' memories of the rift event were completely scrambled, possibly as a subconscious choice. He didn't want to deal with what the Beast had done to his wife so he had discarded his own memories of the event. That created a broken, insane narrative where he wasn't at fault for being on the road that day. It was an insanely twisted set of logic, but looking at Frank Owens, insane seemed to be where he was mentally.

I tried to talk Owens down even as Olivia scaled the last car, putting her directly above him. Frank must have noticed my distraction, because he looked up just as Olivia was descending upon him feet-first. There was a sudden popping sound accompanied by a flash of mana, and Olivia landed on the scaled back of the Beast instead of Frank Owen's human body. The giant lizard-cat thing leapt forwards and she was thrown by the sudden movement and onto the ground. I pulled the trigger on the pistol and only got a dull click in response. Damnit. I had forgotten that I had run the clip dry before the melee had started. The Beast curved around to reach Olivia and I pulled into myself for the power of the void predator. Part of me screamed that it couldn't possibly be a smart idea to let it out like this for so long, but I wasn't going to lose Olivia if I could prevent it.

The connection between myself and the void spirit flooded back. It screamed in my head with hatred for the Beast. I tried to hold back, but our legs took off at a sprint straight at the Beast. That was wrong, the void spirit was pushing hard and was determined to kill the Beast in a head-on assault. We weren't working together and our identities stayed separate as I was regulated to a passenger in my own body. I tried to leap to the side, but my legs snapped back on course towards the target. Come on, I thought, we are smarter than this. I doubled my efforts to force my way back to control.

The Beast lunged forward and we slid under the incoming jaws. The void-predator yelled and a threatening roar escaped our lips. *We will not be denied this time! You restrict, attack from the wrong angles. We will face this challenge!*

I shouted back at it; *we'll lose your stupid challenge if you go head on!*

Losing is inevitable. We will die in fury and rage.

I finally understood what was happening. The challenge, as the void predator put it, wasn't one it thought it could win. Instead it was lashing out like a cornered animal, desperately hoping that the sudden assault would somehow give it the edge. A second slash from our enemy was only partially dodged and I could feel the hot pain of the wound as we rolled away. The spirit launched us forward for another attack, but the Beast instead body slammed us into a nearby junk pile. Pieces of metal debris and corroded rust fell around and on top of us. We were trapped.

For the first time since we had joined, the void spirit screamed in fear. It was a primal sound of terror and loss as it finally encountered a situation that none of its instincts had prepared it for. I was overwhelmed with the panicking terror for a moment while we heard the sound of the Beast digging its way through the rubble pile it had just made. In any moment it would uncover us and we'd be the latest victim to reside in the Beast's gullet. I fought with my other half and found its hold on my body had weakened as it panicked. I tried speaking to it even as I fought to wrestle control of my body back. *This isn't the plan*, I argued. *We just needed to work together for once in our lives and I could pull us through this.*

It wailed, *You can't! You are a flesh thing, what can you do against a predator? It will get to us soon!*

Something interrupted the digging of the Beast and I took the opportunity to test my control. I had some control over my arms, but my legs were firmly under the control of the panicking spirit, kicking wildly in an attempt to run. I tried to think soothingly at the void-spirit.

I can get us out of this, I thought, *but I need your abilities. Just work with me for once instead of fighting me and we can get this done.*

The words came back in an almost spiteful tone, *Why should I?*

That was dangerously close to a logical response from the thing in my head. I gave it the simplest, most appealing argument I knew of for it. I thought, *If I fail at least we'll die fighting instead of trapped inside this rubble. Would you rather die meeting the challenge or being casually eaten?*

There was a hesitant moment as the void-spirit considered my words and weighed them against its own hatred to give up control. I slowly felt my legs return to my control as I began to examine my surroundings. My unusual eyesight isn't dependent on light like normal people, but is excellent at determining depth and I was able to figure out that there were only a couple inches of debris plus a torn car door between myself and the outside world. I could hear a fight still going on the other side, so we would have to hurry. The void-predator had fed well during the melee and I pulled on the excess amounts of power that it had. During the ambush and today's melee, the spirit had been able to partially phase our body into the stuff of the void. It was an easy way for it to reduce the damage we took and blur our outline, but I decided to take it to the next level. I let the void-stuff run throughout my entire body and focused on phasing into that other state of being.

I tried not to panic as I thought about my reluctant ally taking over at this point and living the rest of my short life as something so utterly non-human. The spirit, still disinterested in joining me mentally as before, was still willing to help and guided me in continuing the phasing. There was a sudden feeling of vertigo as the world of gravity and physics lost some control on me and my relationship with the physical world suddenly became very complex. I could actually feel light passing through me, feeling the sparse light particles like a normal person might feel a stiff breeze. The physical debris became a merely uncomfortable obstacle that I could push through like a wad of gel. The weirdest part was that my feet stayed on the ground. It took me a moment to realize I had to will myself to pass through solid object. I figured so as long as I didn't try the same stunt with Mother Earth, I should be able to avoid falling where gravity wanted to pull me. Even gravity felt different. You never really notice the effect gravity has on you until it's not there anymore. It felt unevenly applied and had the momentary flashback of swimming in the void-stuff as the spirit must have done years or even decades before we met. There was a sense of wistfulness from the void-predator as it found our body feeling more like itself ever since we had first unwillingly joined.

I pushed through the debris and found myself in what was probably the biggest fight of my career thus far. One of the SWAT team members had pulled Chauncey out of the way and applied first aid, but their bullets were clearly having no more effect than mine had before. There were a couple bloody rips in the beast's hide where Olivia's revolver had torn chunks of meat away, but the revolver was nowhere to be seen. A quick glance showed that Olivia had been the one to distract the Beast from digging my butt out of the collapsed stack, but had paid a terrible price for it. Her uniform was rent in several places, with only the bulletproof vest underneath having prevent worse damage. The Beast was chewing on her arm, apparently unable to snap it off like it wanted. A dull brass-like metal showed through in several places and I realized I was seeing what passed for her internal skeleton. She was clearly in a lot of pain, but still trying to punch the Beast in the head with her working arm. Staying in this phased state was exhausting for both of us, but I needed the protection for just a little bit longer. The Beast must have seen me out of the corner of its eye because it whipped its tail out straight at my face. I phased through the offending limb and dropped to the ground, scurrying right between its legs. I dug around behind my back and pulled out the 50 caliber pistol I had bought from James. I pressed the barrel against the surprisingly amble reproductive organs I found there and uttered a quick apology to my own gender as I pulled the trigger repeatedly.

I had originally scoffed when James had offered to sell the firearm to me. I didn't even own a spare clip for it and the .50 caliber rounds were stupidly long, being the same as used on some large game rifles. I had meant to simple pick up one of those large game rifles, but James sold me on the thing when he pointed out the unique ammunition he had made for the long-barreled monstrosity. Each bullet had been meticulously engrammed with twin spells and charged with a surprising amount of mana. Each round had cost me forty dollars apiece, but damn if the effect wasn't worth every penny.

The first spell effect activated once the bullet left the gun, doubling the kinetic force and driving the titanium plated bullet right through the lizards' testicles and into the body cavity beyond. Once that kinetic force was spent, the second set of spell engrams activated and a sound like a muffled thunderclap echoed from the poor animal's bowels. I was sprayed with blood and offal as the second spell sent a ripping kinetic force that propelled pieces of the bullet and bones through the things lower body. The incredibly dense musculature of the Beast prevented it from being a killing blow, but like with Chauncey, such dramatic damage has a way of putting the target in a state of shock. I rolled to the side and let the phasing pass, putting me completely back into the real world. The weight of proper gravity and physics descended on me and I almost passed out right there from the sudden change. Instead, I quickly ejected the magazine and slipped in one last bullet I had kept in my pocket. I walked right up to the dazed Beast's head and put the barrel up against the soft pallet in its upper jaw. The eyes were still unfocused, but the hate and madness in them still glared out against a world both it and Frank Owens wanted to see punished. I looked straight into one of those eyes and whispered, knowing that somewhere in the FeyWilds Frank Owens could hear me.

"I'm sorry about your wife, Frank, and I'm sorry about this too."

I turned my head and pulled the trigger. There was another fierce kickback and another thunderous whump as the round discharged. One of the eyes popped and the other filled with blood. Blood leaked form the Beast's nose and jaws and the whole body went slack. I waited a moment to see if it would disappear and be replaced by Frank Owens, but nothing happened. Damn it, that meant I hadn't just killed the Beast, but doomed Frank Owens to a brief and terror filled life in the indomitable danger of the FeyWilds. I had hoped that wouldn't be the case but had been prepared to accept the price on my consciousness. I kicked the head of the Beast once out of sheer spite and then fell down next to my partner in an exhausted heap. Her eyes were glazed over with pain and exhaustion, but she still managed to turn her head towards me. "Did we get it?"

"We did," I confirmed.

She looked at the tattered remains of her arm. "Then it was all worth it."

"Damn straight," I said and then lapsed into

semi-consciousness as the still standing members of Mhanke Heights Police department moved in.

Chapter 34

I woke up some time later in the hospital. I was amused to note that I was in the same room that had previous held Abigail Smithson. She must have been discharged because I didn't see her around. I couldn't help but to briefly glance down at my wrists to make certain they weren't bound like hers had been. Chauncey lay in the next bed, his chest looking to be more bandage than skin. He was asleep and I didn't blame him. I hit the nurse call button, dreading a visit from Bambi, but was surprised to see that it was Mike Al-Radke and Olivia that walked in. Mike looked like a half-dressed mummy, with bandages over his right chest, top of his head and in several places on his leg. He seemed to be moving ok, but it was clear he had been in the thick of things during the combat. Olivia's shredded arm was wrapped in a layer of bandages, with the proportions just enough off to remind me of the missing flesh.

That concerned me and I pointed out the injured limb. "Is that arm going to be ok? It got pretty badly worked over."

Olivia shrugged, but I noticed that one

shoulder raised higher than the other. "It'll regrow so long as I eat a little more than normal. Probably be ok in a dozen days, tops."

I looked over at my hospital companion. "How about Chauncey?"

There was a momentary pause/ "He got a rough tally of internal injuries, but the shooting wasn't fatal. They are going to have to regrow part of his liver. " He sighed and ran a hand through his thinning hair. "I've never heard of that technology before, so I just hope it works."

Images of Chauncey laying bloody in the dirt came unbidden to my mind. I swallowed. "I hope so too. Any idea what I'm in for?"

"Well, for starters it's been 12 hours since you passed out and the hospital doesn't normally discharge the unconscious. Follow that up with several cuts that required stitches, some broken ribs and a bullet hole and you are going to be in here for at least tomorrow."

I winced. "Think I'll get out by Friday night?"

He laughed. "I'll see what I can arrange. In the meantime, I did want to talk to you about the case. Olivia? Can you excuse us for a minute?"

She nodded. "I got to go pick up my sister anyways. She's been freaking out since the news reported on the firefight and I don't want to worry her more." With that, Olivia turned around and strode out of the room.

I looked after her. "Must be nice not to need hospital stays."

Mike shook his head ruefully. "The doctors couldn't figure out if she needed one or not, so it was her call. She's got enough staples in her to set off even the most obtuse metal detector."

"You didn't mention the SWAT team. Did we…" I paused for a moment, afraid of the answer.

"Three of ours died. Another officer in critical condition. Judy broke a couple teeth, but they were probably implants she's broken before. The woman never shies from a punch." Mike grabbed one of the plastic chairs from a corner of the room and sat down, finally looking as tired as he must have felt. He spoke again, "For the Coven, they lost almost a dozen men and have two in critical. John Hernandez's employees lost two and had two more survive. The remaining eight gang members are all in custody, awaiting transfer to the state ERC holding facility and trial."

"Abigail?"

"She's home. We've had 2 more girls and a teenage boy show up with different stages of Ardetha treatments. Only one is in the reversible stage, but none are full-fledged. They'll likely be given counseling and be released on their own recognition. It's not ideal, but there's no proof of a crime beyond their condition. We'll have to keep an eye on them to make certain they don't get those additional treatments."

I nodded. It wasn't an ideal situation, but that seemed to be the nature of ERC work. "It's the best we can do, I guess. I hope they find a way to adjust. Is it all over? Frank gone, John Hernandez dead?"

He nodded. "Looks that way. Not certain who was the initial contact on the coven side, but John is gone and that removes their way in. Frank Owens hasn't shown up, but with the Beast dead, we'll probably never know what happened to him."

I looked down at the hospital bed. "It doesn't feel like a closed case. No one got arrested aside from the coven survivors. People are still hurt by everything that happened and that is not going away."

Mike put a hand on my shoulder. "Sometimes it doesn't get to be a clean close like that. The gangs will start fighting over the convoy area and no one knows how the other Ardetha covens will take the loss. We did stop the murders though and prevented the Ardetha trade for the time being."

"I suppose it'll have to be enough."

He laughed. "Don't worry. Not all of our cases are big dramatic messes like this one. Most are just normal cop stuff with a little mana-tech thrown in.

Monday, you and Olivia get to interview all our newly-registered Ardetha kids for documentation purposes. I promise tons of eye rolling and heavy sighs whenever you repeat a question."

I chuckled, then groaned as my stitches complained. "That actually sounds pretty acceptable."

"You and Olivia really did do great work out there. You figured out Frank Owens and she managed to keep you and Chauncey alive when it counted. I'm glad to have you on the team."

He paused a moment and grabbed a package from the back of the room. I opened the box and laughed as my hands passed over a solidly built braille keyboard. "It reminds me of something I never got around to saying; Welcome to Mhanke Heights, Detective Marcus."

I smiled at the words. I was part of Mhanke Heights now. I'd bled for it, fought for it and would keep doing so as long as I could.